A Girl Called Tommie

By
Thelma G. Norman

TEACH Services, Inc.
P U B L I S H I N G
www.TEACHServices.com

Copyright © 2004 TEACH Services, Inc.
ISBN-13: 978-1-57258-291-0
Library of Congress Control Number: 2004109731

Published by

TEACH Services, Inc.
PUBLISHING
www.TEACHServices.com

Contents

Too Much Molasses 5

Naughty—Part of the Time 11

City Girl in the Country 15

A One-Bird Circus 26

Thanksgiving and Gift Giving 33

Red Spots Among the Brown 40

Sudden Storm 47

Spitzie's Practical Joke 56

Beauty in a Jar 63

Tommie's Painful Lesson 67

Molasses in a Shoe 75

Sunday School on Saturday 83

Winter in the Ozarks 92

Only One Loyal Friend 99

School Buses Won't Wait 109

A Baby in the House 118

Prayer and a Surprise 127

A Promise of Something Better 132

Bud and Tommie took turns sticking their fingers into the can of thick molasses. It was delicious, but they hoped Mamma wouldn't find out!

Too Much Molasses

The back door slammed behind Tommie as she ran down the gray stone steps. She looked around for her little brother and saw him stacking wood beside the barn.

"Come on, Bud!" she called. "Mamma said we can go to Mr. Willis's mill and get some molasses." She swung a tin bucket in her hand.

Tommie liked to go to the mill because she could play with Mr. Willis's little girl Margaret. They had fun together, especially when Margaret took her to watch the molasses being made.

"You children can play at the mill, but be sure you're back in time to bring home the cows," Mother said.

"We'll be back in time," called Tommie. She and Bud started down the road.

"And Tommie—"

"Yes, Mamma?"

"Be sure you help Bud carry home that gallon of molasses. Don't wait until you're almost home before you take the bucket from him and then pretend you've carried it all the way!"

"All right, Mamma," Tommie said in a small voice. She felt ashamed and wondered how Mamma knew about that. Mamma must be smarter than she thought.

The summer sun shone hot over the Ozark Mountains. The children stepped quickly down the dusty road, careful not to cut their bare feet on the sharp stones. Three times they had to wade through a little creek that ran back and forth across the road. How good the cold water felt to their hot feet!

When they reached the Willis home, Tommie handed the molasses bucket to Mrs. Willis and then ran out to play with Margaret.

"Let's go down to the mill and watch Daddy," Margaret suggested. "Bud's probably never seen molasses made. Have you, Bud?"

"No, but I would sure like to," he said.

At the mill, the three children watched Mr. Willis. He pushed long stalks of sugarcane through wooden rollers which squeezed out the cane juice. A mule hitched to the rollers walked slowly in a big circle to keep the rollers turning, and the juice from the cane stalks ran into large shallow pans set over a fire. Margaret's four big sisters stood by the pans stirring the juice as it bubbled and boiled. How good it smelled! When it became thick and gooey and a dark-brown color, they poured it into buckets like Tommie had brought.

Margaret handed Tommie and Bud each a piece of cane stalk that had been pressed through the rollers. She told them to dip the feathery end into the foaming syrup and then lick it off. U-m-m-m, it was delicious! Tommie loved molasses. Her family teased her by saying she would eat it on almost *anything*, even fried eggs.

When the time came to start home, Mr. Willis handed Tommie her bucket filled with warm molasses.

"Tell your mother that this molasses was made from that load of cane your daddy brought in this week," said Mr. Willis. "It sure turned out good!"

"Thank you, Mr. Willis. We'll remember to tell her. Good-bye! Good-bye, Margaret," said Tommie.

Taking turns carrying the bucket, Tommie and Bud walked down the road. When they came to the first place where the creek crossed the road, they sat down on the bank and dangled their feet in the water.

"I wonder what this molasses is like," said Tommie. "Mr. Willis thought it turned out real good, and I'm going to look!"

"Will Mamma care?" asked Bud.

"She didn't say not to." Tommie took the lid off the bucket. Some of the molasses dripped from the lid and Tommie caught it on her finger.

"Oh, it is good!" she said, licking her finger. "It is the best molasses I've ever tasted!" Carefully she scooped off all the molasses on the bucket lid and ate it.

"I want some, too," Bud said.

"Well, there's a whole bucketful," Tommie told him.

Bud hesitated, then stuck his finger into the bucket and licked it off. Tommie did the same. A few minutes later Tommie said, "We'd better not eat too much of this. Mamma might not like it."

"If you don't want her to find out, you'd better wash your face," said Bud. "It has molasses all over it."

"So has yours!"

After washing their faces in the cold creek, Tommie and Bud hurried on. Before long they came to the second place where the creek crossed the road.

"I'm going to have just one more taste of that molasses," said Tommie.

"Then I am, too," replied Bud.

But one taste was not enough, and then minutes passed by the time they replaced the bucket lid, washed their faces, and went on.

Half a mile from home they reached the third creek crossing. Tommie sat down and opened the molasses.

"You'd better not eat any more of that, Tommie," Bud warned. "That bucket doesn't look as full as it did!"

"I'm not going to eat very much," Tommie said. "Anyway, we haven't eaten enough that anyone can tell."

"Mamma can tell, you wait and see," Bud said. But when Tommie didn't stop eating, he joined her.

"Bud, what do you like best made from molasses?" Tommie asked between licks.

"Taffy, I guess."

"I think I like best those big, soft molasses cookies Mamma makes—or maybe gingerbread."

"And you like it on cornbread, and on pancakes, and on biscuits, and you like to lick it off your fingers, and you even like it on fried eggs," Bud teased.

"I do not eat it on fried eggs," protested Tommie, "and I get tired of everybody saying I do!"

"Anyway, there isn't going to be enough molasses left in here for anything if we don't quit eating it!"

By now the molasses had sunk enough in the bucket so anyone could see the bucket was not full. Tommie and Bud washed their faces again and started home. Tommie wondered what Mamma would say when she opened the bucket. She tried to tell herself that Mamma hadn't said not to eat the molasses. But she knew that Mamma probably would have told them not to if they had asked.

As they walked into the yard Tommie said, "Here, Bud, you take the molasses to Mamma while I go after the cows."

Bud's face set stubbornly. But before he could reply, Tommie changed her mind. She felt ashamed because she had meant for him to face the blame alone. "Never mind, I'll take it in!"

"I'll go with you," he said.

Mother took the bucket and opened it at once, just as Tommie had expected.

"Mr. Willis said to—to tell you the molasses was made from that load of cane Daddy brought in this week. He said—he said it turned out real good," Tommie explained. What would Mamma say because the bucket was not full? Surely she could guess what had happened.

Mamma dipped a spoonful of molasses from the bucket and let it pour slowly back, seeing how dark and thick it looked.

"Mr. Willis is right! I don't know when I've seen better molasses," she said. Turning to Tommie she continued, "You'd better run and get the cows. It's getting late. I'll make some biscuits for supper and we'll have them hot with some of this good molasses. You'll like that, won't you, Tommie?"

"Ye—ye—yes, Mamma," stammered Tommie. Perplexed, she hurried away to find the cows. Hadn't Mamma noticed the bucket wasn't full? Somehow, Tommie didn't feel quite right. In fact, she wasn't at all happy. Suddenly she had a horrible thought. Suppose Mamma thought Mr. Willis had cheated and not given them their full gallon of molasses! Tommie decided she'd have to tell the truth as soon as she got back to the house.

The cows weren't hard to find; and as soon as she had them inside the barn lot, she ran to the house to talk to Mamma. As she stepped into the back porch, she heard the man from the neighboring farm talking to Mamma in the living room.

"... one of the funniest things I've seen in a long time." He was chuckling. "I heard these voices down by the creek so I went down to see what was going on. There sat Tommie and Bud with a bucket of molasses between them. First one and then the other would stick a finger into the molasses and lick it off, and they were so busy talking they never did see me. Finally they washed their faces real carefully and went on toward home!" He laughed heartily. "It was funny; it really was!" Then he said more seriously, "Tell your husband I'm sorry to have missed him today. I'll try to get in touch with him tomorrow."

"I'll tell him, Mr. Pender," Mother said. "Good-bye."

Tommie hurried in through the kitchen. "I was coming in to tell you, Mamma," she cried. "Really I was! I was afraid you'd think Mr. Willis had cheated you!"

"Why, Tommie, I know Mr. Willis wouldn't cheat anyone! I just thought he hadn't made enough molasses from our cane yet to give me a full gallon," Mamma said. "But, Tommie, I'm proud of you for not letting someone else be unjustly suspected of dishonesty, even if it meant punishment for yourself. Yes, you'll have to be punished. You, too, Bud," Mamma added as Bud came into the kitchen. "As long as this gallon of molasses lasts, neither of you will be allowed to have any of it. That seems a fitting punishment!"

"That's a worse punishment for Tommie than for me," Bud said. "She likes molasses more than I do!"

"Yes, she does," agreed Mamma, "but if I know my children, and I think I do, Tommie first took the lid off the bucket and tasted the molasses, right?"

"Yes, Mamma, I did. I guess the punishment is fair enough," Tommie said sadly.

Tommie thought the rest of the family would never finish that bucket of molasses. When she mentioned this, Mamma only smiled and said that without Tommie's help a gallon of molasses would always last a long time.

But finally the day did come when Mamma scraped the last of the molasses from the bucket. She washed the bucket and handed it to Tommie.

"Here, Tommie, go get another gallon of molasses from Mr. Willis. If the bucket is still full when you get home, you'll have hot biscuits and molasses for supper." Mamma smiled.

About two hours later, Tommie walked into the kitchen and handed the heavy molasses bucket to Mamma. Mamma carefully opened it, and thick, dark molasses dripped from the lid into the full bucket. Tommie had not even opened the lid.

Naughty—Part of the Time

Tommie remembered her experience with the molasses for a long time. She wondered if other girls had as much trouble being good. Were other girls ever tempted to let younger brother take all the blame for shared mistakes? One day she decided to talk to Mamma about it.

"Mamma, you know the day Bud and I ate the molasses? Well, I was going to let him take the molasses in to you while I went for the cows. Then if you were angry, I'd be gone for a while and maybe it wouldn't be so bad when I got back!"

"But you didn't, did you?" Mamma smiled. "You brought the bucket in yourself."

"Oh, yes," said Tommie. "I changed my mind before Bud even had a chance to refuse. But I feel so ashamed for even having thought of it. Are other girls that naughty?"

Mother threw back her head and laughed. "Oh, Tommie, Tommie!" she said. "You just reminded me of something I hadn't thought about in years! Once I nearly let my little brother take the blame for something I had done. It—"

"You, Mamma?" Tommie interrupted. "But—I never dreamed you were ever naughty when you were a little girl!"

"All little girls are naughty part of the time, Tommie," said Mamma, still smiling. "Now when you have little girls of your own and tell them you ate some molasses you were supposed to take home and were tempted to let your little brother take the blame, I guarantee they will be surprised too."

"But, Mamma, what was it you did that was so naughty?" asked Tommie.

"When I was a little girl," Mamma began, "I was very much like you are today, Tommie. I was a tomboy and fond of rough games. I liked to be out in the woods tramping around. Things that interested other girls did not appeal to me. My sister, your Aunt Bonnie, was different. She was every inch a lady."

"She still is," observed Tommie. "But so are you, Mamma."

"Thank you, Tommie. However, Bonnie was born a lady, and I had to learn it by hard experiences."

"As I seem to be doing," reflected Tommie.

"You're learning, though, Tommie. Our father was a surveyor whose work kept him away from home a great deal. He loved us and never came home without a gift for each of his four children. One evening he came home bringing presents as usual. I don't remember what he brought the rest of us, but he gave Bonnie the most beautiful doll I had ever seen. I'd never been interested in dolls before, but this one fascinated me. To begin with, it was a wooden doll with beautifully painted features and hair. The arms, legs, and neck moved—something we had never seen. And the clothes it wore—I'd never seen anything like them, either. They were of calico, with lace and ruffles and all sorts of frills, even a real hoop in the skirt.

"Bonnie named the doll 'Peggy.' She told me never to touch Peggy because I'd break her for sure. I begged and pleaded to hold her for just one minute. I promised to wash my hands so I wouldn't get the lovely clothes dirty. I told Bonnie over and over how careful I'd be, but she wouldn't give in. Furthermore, she said, if she ever found me touching her doll she'd give me a good spanking!"

"Would she really have spanked you; Mamma?"

"Oh, yes, Tommie. Bonnie was four years older than I and was allowed to spank the younger ones in the family because she was left in charge so often. Whenever Mother was called to help with sickness in the community, she left us with Bonnie."

"Mamma, please go on," begged Tommie. "Isn't there more?"

"Well, I watched and waited, and one day my chance came. Bonnie went to play with friends on the other side of town, but for some reason she didn't take the doll along as usual. I watched until Bonnie was out of sight and then ran to get the doll.

"I had a grand time. I chose a beautiful red gown and put it on her, rocked her, and sang to her; and I wondered why I'd never thought dolls were fun before. Then I began to move her arms and legs and head, making her lie flat, sit up straight, and turn her head. I turned her arm around and around in circles.

"Suddenly, to my horror, doll arms, legs and head began to roll in every direction! They had all been fastened to a big rubber band inside the body, and the band had broken. I had probably put too much strain on it as I played.

"I stood for a moment, stunned. Then an idea flashed into my mind. I gathered up the pieces of the doll and fitted them back together as best I could on Bonnie's bed in the room we shared. When I was finished, no one could have told that the doll wasn't just as Bonnie had left her.

"I was in the room when Bonnie came home. She looked at the doll and then said to me, 'It's a good thing you didn't touch Peggy while I was gone. It would have been just too bad for you if you had!'

"Before I could reply to that, our baby brother, your Uncle Bill, came toddling into the room. He was about three years old. With a sudden lunge he threw himself onto Bonnie's bed and those doll parts flew high into the air. Bonnie and Bill both stared speechless, Bill frightened, Bonnie furious.

"'She won't spank Bill,' I said to myself. 'She's always easy with him because he's the baby.' But I hadn't reckoned with Bonnie's great love for her doll.

"When Bonnie finally found her voice, I'd never heard her so angry. 'Billy, I'm going to give you the worst spanking you ever had in your life,' she shouted. Then she grabbed him, and Billy began to cry. That was more than I could take. Just as she lifted her hand to begin, I jumped forward and snatched him away, screaming, 'Don't you spank him! I did it—I broke your old doll!'

"'You did not! I saw Billy do it! Now get away and let me spank him,' Bonnie snapped.

" 'I broke her first,' I explained, still holding Billy. 'I put her back on the bed so nobody would know I did it, but I'm not going to let you spank Billy for something I did!'

"'Then you'll be spanked for what you did,' Bonnie answered; and I was!"

"Did she spank you hard, Mamma?" Tommie asked.

"Oh, yes. Bonnie's spankings were always worse than those my parents gave. Still, I didn't mind this particular spanking as much as some of the others. I knew I doubly deserved it."

Tommie thought a moment, then mused aloud, "So that's why mothers understand children—it's because they did the same kind of things when they were small."

"I expect it is," Mamma chuckled.

"And is that why you knew I sometimes made Bud carry the molasses bucket until we got nearly home and then pretended I'd carried it the whole way?" asked Tommie.

"Yes," answered Mamma. "That used to be one of my tricks too."

"Well," thought Tommie to herself, "if Mamma was that naughty when she was a girl, but is so good now, maybe there is hope for me if I try hard."

City Girl in the Country

"Tommie, I want you to take a jar of these strawberry preserves down to Granny this afternoon," Mamma said one day after dinner.

"May I go, too?" asked Bud.

"Yes," said Mamma, "if you come home in time for evening chores."

Granny beamed when Tommie handed her the preserves. "I'll make cornmeal pancakes for breakfast in the morning, she said. "They taste delicious with strawberry preserves."

Tommie had hoped that Granny would have time to sing for her. Granny knew all the old Civil War songs, both Union and Confederate. But today Granny had more exciting things to say.

"We have new neighbors, Tommie. They moved into that house across the road and down the hollow. They have a girl about your age named Lucinda."

"Have you seen her, Granny? Do you think she will want to be friends?" asked Tommie.

"Yes, I've seen her. She's a nice little girl. You'll meet her in a few days, probably," Granny replied.

"Where are they from?" asked Tommie.

"From some large city. I don't remember which one. Why don't you run and ask Grandpa? He's down by the barn."

Tommie and Bud raced down the hill to the barn. They could hear voices. As they rounded the comer of the barn, they saw Grandpa talking to a pleasant-looking man. A girl about

Tommie's age was holding the man's hand. Tommie and Bud stopped. They weren't used to strangers.

"Come on, Bud and Tommie," Grandpa called. "Here's a new playmate for you. Her name is Lucinda."

"Hello, Lucinda," both children said together.

"Hello," answered Lucinda. Then she asked uncertainly, "Which one is Tommie?"

"I am." Tommie laughed, her shyness melting away.

Lucinda smiled in return. "I never heard of a girl named Bud, but I never knew a girl named Tommie, either."

"Lots of people think it's strange, but I'm used to it by now," said Tommie. "Why don't you come and play with us?"

Lucinda looked at her father. "Go ahead, Lucinda," he said. "It will be nice for you to make new friends right away."

"I'm going to the spring for a drink first," said Tommie. At the spring, she threw herself flat on her stomach and drank deeply. The walk from home had made her thirsty. When she finished drinking and sat up, she caught Lucinda staring at her.

"Is that—is that the way you always drink?" she asked Tommie.

"Usually," admitted Tommie. "But if you don't want to lie down on your stomach to drink, you can dip the water up in your hands, like this," and, cupping her hands, she filled them with water and drank again.

"But that water comes out of a hole in the ground," said Lucinda. "Are you sure it's clean?"

"Of course it is," replied Tommie. "We learned in school that water that has flowed over sand for a long distance is pure and good to drink. Grandpa says this water has probably come underground for miles. See how clear it is?"

"Yes, only back home our water came out of faucets."

"I've seen faucets at school," said Tommie, "but I like this way of getting water better. Anyway, you'll have to get used to spring water. Nobody has faucets here. The house you've moved into has its own spring." She reached out and picked a sprig of watercress. She liked its crisp, tangy taste.

Lucinda gasped. "Do you eat weeds and things? I mean, won't things like that make you sick?" She pointed to the watercress.

"This is watercress," explained Tommie. "It's good. Haven't you ever seen any before?"

"Mother used to buy watercress in the market sometimes," Lucinda said, "but I didn't know it just grew wild like this."

Tommie handed Lucinda a bit of the plant. "Here, try some."

Lucinda tasted it. "Why, it's not bad. It's better than what Mother bought."

"That's because it's fresh," said Tommie. "Now when your mother wants it she can just come and pick it."

"Will anybody care? Who will we pay for it?"

"It's free, all you ever want." Tommie laughed again. This girl certainly didn't know much about the country.

"What do you do for fun back here so far from town?" Lucinda asked abruptly. Plainly, the question had been bothering her.

"That's no problem," answered Tommie. "Bud and I help on the farm, and that doesn't leave a lot of time to play, especially when there's planting or harvesting to be done. But we still have a lot of fun!"

"Where's the nearest playground with a jungle gym and merry-go-round?" Lucinda asked.

"Jungle gym? I've never seen a playground with a jungle gym," replied Tommie.

"Oh, no," cried Lucinda. "At home even our schools had playgrounds with jungle gyms. Do you ever go to the park to play?"

"There's a state park about twenty-five miles from here, but I've never been there," said Tommie.

"But what do you do?" persisted Lucinda. "At home I could roller-skate on the sidewalk, or in the park. Here there isn't even any sidewalk!" Tears came to her eyes.

Tommie stood up. "Come with me and I'll show you how we have fun. First, let's take a walk in the woods."

"The woods? I'm scared of the woods," protested Lucinda. "What if we meet a bear?"

"I've never seen a bear in my whole life," laughed Tommie.

"Not even in a zoo?"

"I've never seen a zoo, either!"

"At home we got to go to the zoo every year," Lucinda said.

"I can show you some animals, and they're not in cages," said Tommie. "They won't scare you either."

Going into the grass a short distance from the spring, she stopped and pulled away a layer of dead grass and fur, uncovering four tiny baby cottontail rabbits in a hole in the ground. "I found them when I was on my way down here today," she explained. "Aren't they cute?"

"Oh, they're darling!" exclaimed Lucinda. "May I hold one?"

"Yes, I think so," replied Tommie. "The mother will probably move them anyway, now that we've found them."

Lucinda cuddled the tiny animal and for a moment her lost, lonely look disappeared. "Could I keep it for a pet?" she asked.

"They die," Tommie said. "I've tried a couple of times to raise one, but Daddy says they aren't hardy enough. It's better to let the mother rabbit care for it."

Lucinda and Tommie put the little rabbits back in the nest and carefully covered them again.

Tommie moved away and Lucinda followed. Tommie paused beside a small bush. Breaking off two twigs, she put one into her own mouth and offered the other one to Lucinda. "This is spicewood," she said. "Chew it and see if you like it."

Lucinda chewed the end of the stick. "It does taste spicy," she agreed.

"Spicewood is the first thing that blooms in the spring," said Tommie. "Here, rub some of the leaves between your hands and smell. Doesn't it smell good?"

"It smells like Daddy's after-shave lotion," said Lucinda.

"Have you ever seen an Indian arrowhead?" asked Tommie.

"In a museum back home."

Tommie grinned. "I've never been inside a museum, but I can find you an arrowhead."

"A real one? To keep?" asked Lucinda.

"Come on—I'll show you," and Tommie started off at a brisk walk.

A few minutes later they came to a plowed field. Through the south end of the field a stream flowed from a spring, and walnut trees arched across it.

"Indians must have camped by this spring," Tommie explained. "Every time Grandpa plows the field, he turns up arrowheads. Help me look for some."

After fifteen minutes of turning over the soft clods of dirt, Tommie had found two arrowheads, flat and well-shaped. "Here, Lucinda, you take these. I've found lots of them before."

"Oh, thank you, Tommie. Do you mind if I send one to my classmates in the school back home?"

"Go ahead," said Tommie. "We might be able to find something else that would interest them too." Then she pointed to a hill behind some trees. "See that little hill? In the early summer I pick wild strawberries there. They are just about as big as the end of my thumb and as sweet as can be."

"Do you find lots of wild food around here?" Lucinda asked.

"Oh, sure," replied Tommie. "Let's see—in the spring we pick wild greens. That's poke and lamb's-quarters and other things I guess you'd—you'd call weeds. We cook them like spinach. They taste good after not having fresh greens all winter. Then we pick wild strawberries, and huckleberries, which are like blueberries. Then later we pick blackberries. We may be able to find a few late blackberries now. Let's go see."

Tommie led the way along the steep hillside pasture. Lucinda stopped beside a plant that had clusters of wine-colored berries hanging from the branches. "Are these blackberries?" she asked.

"No, that's poke," answered Tommie. "Those berries aren't good to eat. They make good ink, though. Let me show you." She picked a few berries and found a smooth flat rock. Then she drew a tree on it, using the poke berries like crayons. They made dark-red marks.

"That's pretty," said Lucinda. "Have you had drawing lessons?"

"No," said Tommie. "I just like to draw."

"You should sign your name to your pictures, " said Lucinda. Tommie laughed. "Mamma says, 'Fools' names, like their faces, are always found in public places.'"

"This is about the least public place I ever saw," Lucinda giggled.

Going on, they came to the blackberry thicket. Bud, who had been trying to catch up with his sister, came running to them.

"Hey, it's too late for blackberries—" But he stopped when Tommie tossed him a fat, shiny berry. Tommie picked a handful and gave them to Lucinda. Then she popped a few into her own mouth.

"Go ahead," Tommie said. "Try one."

"Are they clean?" Lucinda hesitated.

"Of course. How could they get dirty up there on the vine the way they are?"

"At home we wash everything," Lucinda said, "but I'll try one like this and see." She put a berry in her mouth. "Those are delicious. I wish I could take some back to Mother and Daddy."

"Wait a minute. I'll fix something for you to carry them in." Tommie picked large, tough leaves from a nearby plant and pinned them together with twigs. "Here, will this do?" she asked. "These are burdock leaves, and I make baskets from them now and then."

"How did you learn all these things, Tommie?" Lucinda asked.

"I've lived in the Ozarks all my life. I just learned them as I grew up, I guess. Daddy teaches me about plants all the time."

After Lucinda had filled the basket, they walked on. Suddenly Lucinda screamed in terror. "Snake! Snake!"

Tommie looked where Lucinda pointed. A tiny green snake, his tongue flickering, lay about two feet from Lucinda. "It's only a little grass snake," explained Tommie as she picked it up.

"Don't bring it close to me," said Lucinda.

"I won't," promised Tommie. "But see, he's harmless. Grandpa says that if one of these little snakes bit you you'd die laughing. He was just teasing, of course."

"But don't snakes bite?" asked Lucinda, edging a little closer.

"Yes, they do—at least some of them do," answered Tommie.

"So don't try handling them until you know more about them. Copperheads and cottonmouth moccasins are poisonous. Blacksnakes and probably others will bite you if they are bothered, but they aren't poisonous. Just remember not to put your hands into the weeds or other places where you can't see, and watch where you walk." Tommie laughed. "It's a good thing Bud was carrying the blackberries we picked for your mother and daddy. You jumped a mile when you saw this little fellow. And I'll bet he was as scared as you were!"

"Impossible," shuddered Lucinda.

Tommie moved a short distance away and put the snake on the ground. He glided soundlessly away into the grass. Tommie started over a wooded hill.

"What's that?" Lucinda asked, pointing to a long, gray, round sack hanging in a tree. "It looks like it's made of paper."

"Try hitting it with a stick and you'll see," suggested Bud.

Lucinda was carrying a stick she'd picked up along the way. She lifted it to strike the object in the tree.

"No, Lucinda! Don't!" cried Tommie, grabbing the stick.

Then Tommie turned to Bud. "You ought to be ashamed , she scolded."You know better than to try to get someone to hit a hornets' nest with a stick!" She looked at Lucinda and explained, "That's a hornets' nest. Hornets are like wasps, only meaner. If we disturbed them they'd come boiling out of there and chase us all the way home, stinging us every step we took. They're awful!"

"I'm sorry, Lucinda," Bud said. "I didn't know you'd really never seen a hornets' nest before."

"I'll know one the next time I see it," Lucinda laughed.

"The first hard freeze will kill all the hornets," said Tommie. "Then we will come and get the nest and you can send it to your classmates at your old school."

At the bottom of a hill they came to some small trees. "Watch, Lucinda," called Tommie. "I'm going to climb one of these trees and show you something that is fun."

"Are you allowed to climb these trees?" Lucinda asked.

"Sure. Why not?" said Tommie.

"At home, in the park, we aren't allowed to," the other girl explained.

"Here we're allowed to climb all the trees we want to. How else are we going to pick persimmons or look into birds' nests?" Tommie asked.

Lucinda lifted her stick to strike the round gray sack hanging in the tree. But Tommie stopped her. "That's a hornet's nest," she explained.

"What are persimmons?"

"Persimmons are fruit," explained Tommie. "They aren't good to eat until after frost. I'll show you some next fall."

Tommie climbed quickly up a small tree. As she neared the top it began to sway. She grabbed a branch with both hands and let go with her feet. The tree slowly bent down until her feet gently touch the ground. Tommie let go and the tree sprang upright again.

"See?" she said. "That was fun. Now you try!"

Lucinda tried and tried and finally managed the trick herself. "This is lots better than a park," she said happily. "What can we do next?"

"We can wade in the creek for a while," Tommie suggested. The water in the creek was clear and only about knee-deep. Bud and Tommie waded into the water, but Lucinda hung back. "I see things in there," she said.

"You mean the minnows, the little fish?" asked Tommie.

"No," replied the other girl. "Funny things, with pinchers."

"Oh, you mean the crawdads. They do look vicious, don't they?" said Tommie with a smile. "But see, they back away from me when I wade toward them. They won't pinch you unless you catch them!"

"I wouldn't touch one of them for anything," Lucinda declared. She waded gingerly into the water. "Oh, this water is cold," she squealed.

A short time later Tommie looked at the sun. It hung low in the sky. "Bud and I are going to have to go home and help with the chores."

"Well, I sure have had fun this afternoon," Lucinda said, "and I really didn't expect to at all. I think I'll learn to like it here with you as my friend, Tommie."

"I've never had a friend my age before who lived this close to me," replied Tommie. "I'm so glad you're here."

Later that evening Tommie told Mamma all about Lucinda. "She's nice, but she certainly doesn't know much," she said.

"You'd be just as lost and lonesome if we moved into a big city," Mamma reminded her.

"Yes, I expect I would," Tommie agreed.

"Be patient with this new friend of yours," Mamma said. "You can teach her our ways, and I venture to say you'll learn quite a bit from her."

Tommie grinned. "I'll be just the kind of friend I'd like to find if we moved to a big city."

A One-Bird Circus

One night Tommie awakened as rain pelted hard against the house. Wind roared through the trees, lightning streaked past the window, and loud thunder rolled through the hills. Tommie pulled the covers over her head and snuggled closer to her little sister, Becky Jane. Thunderstorms scared Tommie, and she hated them. It did no good for Daddy to explain that thunder never hurt anyone, and that the long lightning rod on the comer of their house helped keep lightning away. She was still afraid. She was glad when the storm passed over so she could go back to sleep.

The next morning the sun shone brightly, but signs everywhere told of the storm. Broken branches lay strewn across the yard, and near the house, a usually dry creek bed was foaming with water.

The fields were too wet to work, so after milking the cows and feeding the chickens and horses Tommie and Bud had time to play. The creek by that time had gone down enough for wading, but Tommie knew most of the water would be gone by midafternoon.

"Let's go and see if the wet-weather springs are flowing," Bud said when they grew tired of wading.

"All right," agreed Tommie.

"Let's go past the barn and cut across from there," said Bud. Before they got far down the road, he pointed to a figure coming toward them.

"Isn't that Lucinda coming?" he asked. "If it is, I'm not going to play with her!"

"Why not?" asked Tommie in surprise.

"Because she's always talking about how much better things were back where she came from, that's why!" he said., "If things were so much better back there, why did they come here?"

"I'm glad she came! It's nice to have a girl my own age to play with," said Tommie. "I'm going to go meet her." Tommie ran down the road.

"Hi, Lu," she called, panting a little from her run.

"Hi, Tommie," replied Lucinda. "See, I brought something for you." She held out her cupped hands. Nestled inside them was a baby blue jay. He was feathered out in bright blue, black, and white, with a tiny topknot on his head. His beady eyes watched them alertly, but he didn't seem frightened.

"Oh, isn't he cute!" squealed Tommie, taking him into her own hands and stroking his soft feathers. "Where did you get him?"

"Your Uncle Bill found him and asked me to bring him to you. He said the little fellow was probably blown out of his nest by the storm last night," explained Lucinda.

"Come on," said Tommie. "I want to show him to Mamma and Daddy!" The two girls hurried to the house, where they showed Tommie's parents the little bird and explained where he came from.

"You won't be able to raise a blue jay, Tommie," said her father. "What would you feed him? Go put him on a lower limb of that chinquapin tree up the hill, and maybe some older jay will come and feed him. I've read of that happening."

Sadly Tommie obeyed. The little bird looked so lonesome sitting on the limb by himself. She hated to leave him there.

After only a short visit, Lucinda had to go home. As Tommie wandered alone in the yard she could hear an occasional plaintive call from the little bird in the tree. Suddenly she thought, "If I could get him to eat, maybe Daddy would let me keep him for a pet!"

Tommie stooped down and searched in the grass. When she stood up again she had what she wanted—a small grasshopper.

Tommie ran up the hill to the little bird, which was perched just as she had left him. He eyed the grasshopper with interest, but wouldn't open his mouth.

"Don't you know you'll starve if you don't eat?" she scolded. "And if you have to be left out here in this tree an owl or a crow will get you for sure. You'd better eat so Daddy will let me keep you!"

Again Tommie offered him the grasshopper. And again and again. But he just wouldn't open his mouth. Finally, almost ready to give up, Tommie said "All right! For the last time, are you going to sit here and starve?" She thrust the struggling grasshopper at him with a quick, impatient move, and to her surprise he opened wide his mouth and gulped it down.

Tommie caught more grasshoppers and then experimented. She found that the little bird would open his mouth for food only if she brought it toward him swiftly or circled it over his head.

Carrying the bird to the house, she showed Daddy how she could get him to eat. "Now may I keep him?"

"I guess so," Daddy answered. "You're going to have to catch a lot of grasshoppers, though."

"I know," Tommie said quickly, "but I don't care. Really, I won't mind a bit!"

"What are you going to call him, Tommie?" Becky Jane asked.

"I've been thinking, and I've decided to call him 'Jason,'" Tommie replied.

But "Jason" did not stick. By the end of the week everyone in the family was calling Tommie's new pet "Jake." As the bird grew older, even Tommie had to admit that "Jake" better suited his personality.

Saucy, mischievous, affectionate, and hungry, Jake delighted the whole family. At first Tommie spent most of her spare time catching grasshoppers, but Jake soon learned to catch them himself. Nor was his diet limited to grasshoppers. He joined the family at their meals, sharing bread and butter, lettuce, cooked vegetables, and fruit. Jake ate his food from a special dish—a lid from a peanut-butter jar.

He performed a one-bird circus, and the family was his audience. As soon as he was full at meals, he would search for places to store the leftovers. He tried to fill Daddy's overall pockets with bread, tuck raisins into Mamma's long black hair, and drop bits of lettuce down the back of Tommie's dress.

While Tommie sat reading in the living room one day, Bud called to her.

"Tommie, come quick! Come see what Jake's doing."

Running to the backyard, Tommie howled with laughter at what she saw. Bud's special pet, a part-Airedale dog named Bob, ran madly around the house, barking as loud as he could. On his back perched Jake, claws gripping the dog's curly hair, delightedly screaming, "Thief! Thief!" at Bob's every bound. And Bud, bent over with laughter, was egging them on.

"Go Bob! Ride 'em Jake!" Tommie joined in. After another circle of the yard, Bob lay down in the shade, panting, and Jake flew to Tommie's shoulder.

"Jake," laughed Tommie, "you're a scoundrel, an out and-out scoundrel! Do you think Bob enjoys playing your horse?"

But following days proved that Bob did enjoy giving Jake "horseback" rides, for seldom a day passed that Jake and his willing steed didn't take at least one fast ride through the yard.

Jake's mischief never got him into very serious trouble, but at least once it did cause him discomfort. That was the day he took a bath in the milk Mamma had set out for the chickens. When the milk dried, poor Jake's feathers stuck together and he was unable to fly. What a fuss he made, hopping, squawking and straining to beat his wings. Tommie heard the commotion and came to investigate. When she discovered what had happened she dunked him in the spring to wash off the milk. Jake shook himself and flew to the top of the big white oak tree that grew by the spring. He sat there preening his feathers and grumbling to himself for the next hour. Never again did he take a bath in milk.

Not all of Jake's language was harsh and screaming. Sometimes he perched on Tommie's shoulder and sang a soft, whispering melody nearly as pretty as a canary's. He sang occasionally for the rest of the family, too, but never for strangers.

As the summer passed into fall, Jake spent much time storing acorns. He flew to the top of the house and patiently wedged acorns up under any loose shingle he could find.

"I wouldn't be surprised to find oak trees growing from the roof next spring," Daddy told Tommie.

November came with sharp, cold nights. One evening as Tommie and Bud went to the barn with Daddy to milk, he said, "From the way it looks, I judge we'll have snow tonight."

Sure enough, when the milking was finished and they stepped out of the barn, big, feathery snowflakes swirled through the air. Entering the yard, Tommie noticed Jake sitting on the window box, protected by the eaves from the falling snow. He was grumbling and talking to himself:

"What's the matter, Jake?" Tommie teased. "Don't you like snow? It won't hurt you!"

The next morning Jake was gone. Tommie called and called, but no fluff of blue-and-white feathers came to perch on her shoulder.

"Where do you suppose he is?" she wailed. "What could have happened to him?"

"I imagine he just migrated south, Tommie," comforted her mother. "He'll be all right!"

"I'll miss him," gulped Tommie. "Do you suppose he'll ever come back?"

"I wouldn't be surprised," answered Mamma, "but we'll have to wait until next spring to find out."

Tommie took the peanut-butter-jar lid from the table and placed it far back in the cupboard, just in case. "It's going to be a lonesome winter without Jake," she thought sadly.

Tommie got up early each morning to inspect her rabbit traps. She hoped her trapline would bring her spending money for Christmas.

Thanksgiving and Gift Giving

One November day Daddy took his tools to the yard and began making long, narrow boxes.

"These are rabbit traps," he explained to Tommie. "I am going to have a trapline this winter. If you children want traps, I'll make them for you. You can earn good spending money trapping rabbits."

"I could use some extra spending money," said Tommie. "Christmas isn't far away!"

"All right, then," Daddy said. "If you have a trapline, you'll have to get up early in the morning to inspect the traps before you go to school. These box traps don't hurt the rabbits, but I don't like animals to be without food and water for any length of time. That's why you can't miss a day of looking at your traps."

"I'll go every day," Tommie promised.

"Then I'll make you six traps, and I'll show you where to set them. When you catch a rabbit, just put him in a gunnysack. I'll sell him when I go to sell mine. Buyers pay twenty-five cents each for them."

Bud wanted traps too, so he and Tommie each had six. One Sunday afternoon Daddy took them out into the fields and showed them places to set their traps. He explained how the traps worked and gave them pieces of apple for bait.

"Daddy," said Tommie, "since I have to go to my traps every day, why can't I wait until I get home from school instead of going early in the morning?"

"Rabbits do most of their feeding and running about at night," Daddy answered. "That's when they will go into your traps, If you take them out in the early morning, they won't be left shut up all day without food or water."

"Oh, I see," said Tommie. She didn't want the rabbits to suffer either.

Daddy warned Tommie and Bud not to be disappointed if they didn't catch any rabbits the first few days. The animals would have to get accustomed to seeing the traps before they would go into them, he said.

The days were getting shorter, and it was still dark in the mornings when Tommie went to look at her traps. She and Bud carried lanterns, and sometimes Bob would go along with one of them for company.

Tommie felt disappointed the days her traps were empty. But other mornings she would find one or two, and once she caught three. The quarters began to accumulate.

Days they didn't have to go to school, Tommie and Bud waited until daylight to inspect their traps. One Sunday Tommie found her first five traps empty, but the door of the sixth trap had fallen closed. She hoped that meant a rabbit had closed it and not just some bird or larger animal had brushed against the trigger and caused the door to fall.

Tommie opened the trap and took a look inside, then closed it quickly. Some kind of animal was curled up in there, but it wasn't a rabbit. Tommie couldn't be sure what it was. She had closed the trap too fast to get a really good look. Would it bite if she tried to get it out?

After debating what to do, she picked up the trap and started home. Since the other traps had been empty, she had nothing else to carry. Putting the trap down outside the kitchen door, she went and told Daddy about it. He looked inside the trap.

"Why, that's a possum, Tommie," he said. "Surely you've seen possums before."

"Yes, I have," said Tommie; "only they look different when they are caught in a rabbit trap. Can you sell him?"

"Sure," said Daddy. "He's worth as much as four or five rabbits, maybe more."

Tommie was glad to hear that. She needed all the money she could get for Christmas.

Thanksgiving vacation came. The day before Thanksgiving Tommie went into the woods and brought back some wild bittersweet vines. The scarlet and orange berries would make a nice centerpiece for the Thanksgiving table. Tommie could hardly wait. Mother always topped Thanksgiving dinner with a big pan of gingerbread served with whipped cream and applesauce. Tommie also looked forward to the little ceremony the family had before dinner when each one named the things he was most thankful for. Tommie already knew what she'd name—her family, trees to swing in, brooks to wade in, the animals in the woods, and molasses!

As soon as Thanksgiving was over Tommie began to spend her spare time poring over the mail-order catalog. She made lists and counted her money until she decided everything was just as she wanted. She had never sent in an order to the mail-order company before, but she knew just what to do. She got an order blank and very carefully and neatly wrote down all the things she wanted: a pretty glass bowl for Mamma, a billfold for Daddy, cups and saucers for Granny and Grandpa, and toys for her brother and Becky Jane. She also ordered two embroidered handkerchiefs for Lucinda.

When she had finished and added up the total, she found she had only a little more than a dollar left. The next morning she left the school bus in town and went to the post office, where she proudly purchased a money order and a stamp. Soon her order sped on its way. A week later the package came.

"Are you going to tell me what's in that package, Tommie?" Mamma asked with a smile.

"It's a secret, Mamma," Tommie explained.

"Oh, tell me, please, please," begged Mamma. "Please tell me!"

Tommie looked at Mamma in surprise.

"Well," laughed Mamma, "that's how you sound whenever I try to keep a secret from you!"

Tommie laughed too. Then she drew herself up in what she considered a dignified manner and said firmly, "I'm sorry, Mamma, you'll just have to be patient!"

Several nights later Mamma said to Tommie, "Let's start making some Christmas candy. Tonight would be a good time to make taffy."

Tommie agreed. So Mamma boiled the molasses, and when it was ready, she poured it onto a big platter to cool. As soon as it had cooled enough, everyone in the family came in to help.

"Be sure to put enough butter on your hands before you start pulling this taffy," Mamma warned. "If you don't, you'll end up with a sticky mess!"

Each one buttered his hands and broke off a big handful of the candy. They pulled the candy into ropes, doubled them, and pulled the lumps out thin again. The taffy turned a pale golden color and began to get hard. Then Mamma broke it into pieces with the handle of a knife. It looked good. Tommie could hardly wait to taste it. Mamma gave each one a piece and put the rest away for Christmas.

The next day, when Tommie came home from school, Mamma said, "I want you to crack some of those hickory nuts you gathered this fall and pick out the meats, Tommie. You'll have time to do it before you go for the cows. I'm going to make some hickory-nut fudge."

Tommie finished with the nuts before time to go for the cows, so she sat down in the living room with a book. Daddy came in with a jar of cream. "Mamma is going to need some butter for the candy she is making tonight.

"Are you going to do the churning, Daddy?" asked Bud.

"Yes, I am," said Daddy. "I'm going to show you that I can get this cream churned without shaking the jar more than one minute."

"Oh, you can't do it in only one minute," said Tommie. "It takes longer than that to churn!"

"You may be right, Tommie," said Daddy, "but I can shake the jar more times in a minute than the rest of you can."

"All right," said Tommie. "Let's count and see!"

Daddy shook the jar and Tommie counted. When the minute was up, Tommie said, "Give me the jar—I can do better than that. You just count and see!"

When Tommie's minute was over, Bud clamored for a turn. He was just as fast as Tommie, but neither of them was as fast as Daddy. Then Tommie tried again. She was sure she could beat Bud if she had another chance, and she did. Bud demanded another chance to beat Tommie. Before his minute was over the cream began to show flecks of butter in it.

"See, Daddy, it takes longer than one minute to make butter," Tommie said.

Daddy laughed. "How long did I shake that jar, Tommie?"

Tommie thought a while. "Just for one minute," she laughed. "Bud and I shook it the rest of the time. That was a pretty clever trick you played on us!"

After supper Mamma made the fudge. Tommie and Bud took turns stirring it. Just before pouring it into the pans Mamma added the hickory-nut meats. When the fudge was cold, Mamma gave each one a piece and put the rest away with the taffy.

The days seemed to pass slowly, but at last Christmas Eve arrived. Everyone hung a big red stocking from the fireplace.

Next morning Becky Jane woke up Tommie. "It's Christmas! It's Christmas!" she squealed. "My stocking is full to the top!"

At that everyone else woke up too, and they began investigating stockings. Each stocking held a big orange and some Christmas candy. Poking out from the top was a bunch of red grapes the children called "Christmas grapes," because Christmas was the only time they had them. Every year, as far back as she could remember, Tommie had found a bunch of grapes in her stocking.

After they all opened the presents and finished the chores, Mamma hurried everyone through breakfast.

"We're going to spend the day with Granny and Grandpa," she said.

"May we take our presents?" Bud asked.

"You may each choose one present to take with you," Mamma said.

Tommie found almost all her aunts, uncles, and cousins gathered at Granny's house. A family tradition allowed the oldest granddaughter present to make a huge fruit salad for Christmas dinner. Tommie watched her cousin Ruth cut up apples, bananas, walnuts, and celery. Then she added marshmallows and whipped cream. Next year Ruth would be away at school, and Tommie would get to make the fruit salad. She felt sure she'd be very grown-up then.

Christmas vacation passed all too quickly for Tommie, and almost before she knew it, school started again.

Tommie came to breakfast with a big grin on her face one day in early February. The plate at her place was turned upside down, and when she peeked under it, a shiny new dime lay there. "Happy birthday, Tommie!" her family shouted.

Tommie's family did not celebrate birthdays with parties and cakes. Instead, the person having a birthday always found a dime under his breakfast plate and was excused from helping with the chores all day.

This birthday proved particularly happy for Tommie. Lucinda gave her a tiny bottle of perfume, and at school her classmates sang "Happy Birthday" to her. A new shipment of library books arrived that day, and the teacher let Tommie have first choice of them. She chose a book called *Under the Lilacs* by Louisa Alcott, and she knew with no chores to do that afternoon she could read and read and read. To Tommie that was far more enjoyable than a party could ever be.

The week after Tommie's birthday her teacher brought a box into the classroom and, asked, "Who wants to trim the valentine box?"

The class chose a committee with Tommie as a member. They trimmed the box with great care. First they covered it with bright-red paper. They glued white crepe-paper ruffles to each corner, and different-sized white hearts on the sides.

For the next few days Tommie's class made valentines during art periods. They drew, cut, pasted, and giggled, using stacks of red construction paper, paste, and lace paper doilies.

Tommie had some money from her trapline, so she bought valentines at the store for Lucinda and her teacher. She made the ones she gave to other classmates. Finally the big day arrived, and as her teacher passed out the valentines, Tommie watched with excitement as a big heap of white envelopes piled up on her desk.

That afternoon, as Tommie went for the cows, she said to herself, I got some awfully pretty valentines today, but the nicest valentine I ever could receive would be to have Jake back." There was just the barest hint in the air that spring might not be long in coming. Would her pet blue jay come, too?

Red Spots Among the Brown

Spring arrived and, with it, sweet-smelling flowers. They bobbed and waved in the soft spring breezes, making the hills a gay patchwork of color. Flowers were underfoot and overhead, and Tommie loved them all—violets, Johnny-jump-ups, bluets, sweet Williams, anemones, buttercups, dogwood, redbud, wild plum, serviceberry, and many others. She stood gazing at them one day before entering the house. Then, remembering that chores waited for her, she ran up the steps, calling, "Mamma! Mamma! I'm home!"

"I'm in the kitchen," answered Mamma.

"Mamma, our class is going to have a flower show tomorrow at school. We are each to make a bouquet of wild flowers. What can I fix that would be different?"

Mamma thought a minute. "The mayapples in bloom down the hollow below the barn are beautiful just now. Why don't you get some of those to arrange with ferns? I saw some ferns growing on the bank by the wet-weather spring."

"That sounds wonderful, Mamma," exclaimed Tommie. "May I go get them right now?"

"Yes, go ahead," answered Mamma. "Becky Jane may go with you if she wants to."

Little Becky Jane hurriedly put away her paper dolls and grabbed Tommie's hand. She was always ready to go with "Sissy," her special name for Tommie. "I want to go," she cried. "And, Mamma, I'm going to pick a big, big bouquet for you!"

"Mamma," said Tommie pleadingly, "it's so nice and warm outside, can't we go barefoot?"

"No, Tommie!" Mamma answered firmly. "You know what your daddy says—when you hear the first whippoorwill call, it's warm enough to go barefoot, and not before. I know the air is warm outside, but the ground is still cold. Now, you and Becky Jane run along and pick your flowers."

Tommie found the mayapple plants without any trouble because their unusual shape made them stand out from the flowers around them. About eight inches from the ground their main stem branched into two smaller stems, each having a pale green, umbrella-shaped leaf at the top. At the point where the stem branched grew a single waxy white flower with a yellow center. The mayapples had a faint sharp odor, very different from the pleasing fragrance of most spring flowers. Daddy, who had studied botany in college, had told Tommie that another name for the mayapple was "mandrake." He said some people used it in medicine. Tommie knew that by summer the mayapple blossoms would turn into green fruit about the size of a quarter. These would ripen into a bright gold in July.

Tommie cut more than enough flowers for her bouquet, trimming off the leaves carefully. Then she and Becky Jane cut across the corner of the pasture to the wet-weather spring. It had been a rainy month, and the spring had formed a small stream that trickled down the hollow.

"Come, Becky Jane, I want to show you something!" Tommie called. Becky Jane, busy picking a big bouquet for Mamma, came quickly when Tommie called.

"I used to do this when I was a little girl like you," Tommie explained as she pulled the cupped, waxy petals from a mayapple blossom and set them afloat in the little stream. "See what nice boats they make?"

Becky Jane took the flowers Tommie offered her and soon had her own fleet of mayapple petal boats bobbing and dancing on the water. Tommie gathered ferns for her bouquet.

When they reached the house, Mamma thanked Becky Jane for her bouquet and then helped Tommie arrange hers. When they were finished, Tommie stepped back and viewed their handiwork with a sigh of satisfaction. Mamma knew just where to put each flower to make it look prettiest.

"That's just lovely," she said softly. "I never would have thought of using just mayapple blossoms and ferns, but they look beautiful together. Thanks for helping me, Mamma!" She sat down and continued, "I'm so tired! I don't know why. A short walk like that never leaves me tired."

"Did you have a hard day at school today?" asked Mamma.

"No," replied Tommie. "That isn't what made me tired. I'm just getting lazy, I guess." She smiled.

Mamma smiled back. "No lazybones are allowed around here," she said. "You'd better gather the eggs, and if you are still tired you may go to bed early tonight."

Tommie did go to bed early, but the next morning she still felt tired. Besides, her head ached. Usually Tommie ate a hearty breakfast, but this morning the sight of oatmeal, home-canned applesauce, and Mamma's good raised bread made her stomach feel strange.

"Tommie, don't you feel well?" Mamma asked.

"I just have a headache."

"I hear several local children have measles," said Mamma. "Maybe that's what is wrong with you, Tommie."

Bud laughed. "'If Tommie had measles, we'd never know it. Her freckles would hide the spots!"

Tommie smiled wanly. She felt too bad to even show her usual resentment at the remark about her freckles.

Mamma looked at her worriedly. "Maybe you'd better stay home from school today, Tommie."

"Oh, Mamma, I can't miss school now!" protested Tommie. "Only three more days of school are left, and I haven't been absent or tardy all year. If I don't get a Perfect Attendance Certificate this year it will be the first time in four years! Besides, there's the flower show today. I'm not really sick, Mamma. I'll be all right."

"Very well, then. I'll let you go," Mamma agreed, "but my better judgment tells me I should keep you home."

The flower show was the first item on the day's schedule. Bright bouquets of wild flowers filled the room. Tommie's creation of green ferns and mayapple blossoms won second place, but she felt too miserable to care. The light and the bright colors of the flowers hurt her eyes, and the aspirin Mamma had given her hadn't helped her headache.

The day dragged on. During the last hour of school the teacher announced, "Today is the last day of school for you sixth graders. Please clean your desks, and I will hand out the Perfect Attendance Certificates. You are getting out of school early because I have to assist with the county seventh-grade exams during the next two days."

Tommie looked at her certificate. The printing blurred before her smarting eyes. "I have my Perfect Attendance Certificate, so now I can go ahead and be sick!" she thought wryly.

Mamma put Tommie to bed as soon as she came in from school. Red spots were beginning to appear on her freckled face. She had the measles. The next five days passed hazily for Tommie. She knew that Mamma spent a great deal of time bathing her feverish body with cool water. And Mamma was always there with a drink when Tommie's mouth felt dry. She cooked Tommie's favorite foods, but Tommie could hardly taste them. She kept the room dark to protect Tommie's eyes, fluffed the pillows, straightened the sheets, and did all she could to make Tommie comfortable. Finally Tommie began to feel better.

On the ninth day Tommie was feeling well enough to get out of bed for a few minutes, so Mamma set her in the big chair in the living room. Becky Jane came dancing in.

"Oh, Sissy, I'm so glad you're better," she cried. "And, Sissy, guess what! Down by the barn—"

Here Mamma scooped Becky Jane up in her arms and put a firm hand over her mouth. "Oh, no, you don't, young lady!" she, exclaimed. "Don't you go telling Tommie the secret we're saving for her!"

"What is it, Mamma—a new calf?" asked Tommie.

"No, it isn't a new calf," said Mamma, "but that is all I'm going to tell you about it. You'll, just have to wait and see!"

"Oh, Mamma," sighed Tommie, "you know I never was very good at waiting."

"Yes, I know," agreed Mamma. "Someday, though, you'll learn patience. Right now you're going back to bed."

Tommie gratefully allowed herself to be put back to bed. She was weaker than she had thought.

That secret kept nagging at her, though. What could it be? It didn't seem fair for everybody to know it when she didn't. All her coaxing and pleading failed to produce even one hint as to what it might be.

"Mamma, don't you know that the suspense about this secret is liable to make me have a setback?" she said one day as Mother was making her bed. "I might get sicker than I was when I first got the measles!"

Mamma laughed. "No chance of a setback now, Tommie, my dear. When a patient gets to the place where he's irritable and saucy he's well on the way to recovery."

Even Tommie had to smile at that. "I'm sorry, Mamma. I'll try not to be impatient, if I can help it."

"In a few days," promised Mamma, "I think you'll be well enough to see this fine secret for yourself."

Sure enough, two days later, as Tommie awakened from a long afternoon nap, Bud came into the room.

"We're going down to the barn to milk, Tommie. Do you want to come along?" he tried to ask casually, but the sparkle in his eyes gave away his excitement.

"I'll be right there," Tommie cried, jumping up quickly. She held onto the bed as the room seemed to tilt and swim. "But not very fast," she added with a grin. "I'm going to go a little slower than usual."

The whole family escorted Tommie down the road toward the barn. She looked around but didn't see anything different. Just as they reached the edge of the barn lot everyone paused and looked at Tommie expectantly. Becky Jane jumped up and down with both hands over her mouth.

"Look up in that peach tree, Tommie," directed Daddy.

Tommie looked. There, not too far up in the tree, a limb held an untidy nest of sticks, and on it sat a bright blue-white-and-black bird whose beady eyes looked fearlessly at her.

"Oh-h-h," breathed Tommie. "Is it—it can't be—"

"It's Jake!" squealed Becky Jane, unable to keep quiet any longer.

"Yes, it's Jake," agreed Daddy. "Or maybe we should say 'Jacquelyn' now. Your Jake turned out to be a mamma blue jay, Tommie. Here, offer him—her—a grasshopper."

He handed Tommie a struggling grasshopper and she pushed it up to the bird. Jake hopped over and ate it. Tommie reached out to stroke her old pet, but Jake jumped away and settled back on the nest. She seemed to be trying to show that she was no longer a carefree pet, but a grown-up bird with heavy responsibilities.

"When Jake's eggs hatch I'll practically be a grandmother to the babies, won't I?" Tommie laughed shakily. She was near tears.

"Well, yes, something like that," Mamma agreed with a smile. "Now I think you'd better come back to the house and rest awhile. You are still weak, and this has been exciting for you."

"I'll say it has," replied Tommie. "I can come back tomorrow, can't I?"

"Yes," said Mamma, "you may."

Tommie looked back over her shoulder as she started up the road back to the house. Jake was settled securely on the nest, back home where she belonged. Tommie had her Perfect Attendance Certificate, she was almost over the measles, and school didn't begin until next September. "It's going to be a wonderful summer," she thought happily.

Sudden Storm

"Granny says she's going back onto the ridge to pick some huckleberries this afternoon," Mamma told Tommie and Bud one morning. "Would you like to go along? I'd like to have enough huckleberries to make a cobbler for supper."

"Oh, yes, I'd like to go! Wouldn't you, Bud?" asked Tommie.

"Sure," said Bud, "only Daddy wants us to finish weeding the garden before we do anything else. About four rows are left, and if we hurry we can get them done before too long."

"When you're through weeding," said Mamma, "dig a few new potatoes and pick some peas. We'll have them for dinner. I think you'll have time to get them."

"All right, Mamma," answered Tommie, and after picking up a bucket for the potatoes and a basket for the peas, the two children started for the garden.

Daddy planted the garden in a different place almost every year. He said it was good to let the land rest, so he let some of the fields on the farm lie unused each summer. This year he chose a spot between the house and the barn for the garden. Tommie was glad because when she got thirsty as she weeded or hoed she could go to the spring for a drink.

Cool breezes chilled Tommie as she and Bud worked on the weeds. But she knew that by midmorning the bright sun would shine hot. They worked as fast as they could to finish the weeding before the sun rose too high in the sky.

After they finished weeding, Bud took a digging fork and dug potatoes while Tommie picked peas. Because the peas climbed up brushy poles Daddy had stuck in the ground for them,

Tommie didn't have to stoop much to get to the plump pods. That was a relief after the weeding.

When they reached the house, Tommie washed the potatoes carefully in the stream below the spring. Then she dropped several handfuls of clean gravel from the stream into the potato bucket and added some water. Taking four or five potatoes at a time, she swished them back and forth, around and around in the bottom of the bucket until the gravel had rubbed off almost all of the potato skins. With a pointed knife she scraped off the remaining tags of peeling, cut out the eyes, and then carried the snowy little potatoes into the house. Mamma put them into a kettle to cook while Tommie sat out beside the spring under the big white oak tree shelling the peas.

When dinner was over, Tommie and Bud each found a bucket and started to Granny's house.

"I may come down after a while and walk back home with you," Mamma said as they left the house. "There doesn't seem to be a breath of air stirring, and a walk might make us feel cooler."

The road was hot, and tiny dust clouds rose under their feet as Tommie and Bud walked along. They took a drink from Granny's spring and cooled their feet in the stream that flowed down the hollow. Then they climbed the path that went up the hill to the house.

Granny had been expecting them. "I'll be ready in a minute," she said. "I'll have to get my bonnet." She looked at Tommie. "Tommie, you forgot your bonnet again, didn't you? I think you'd forget your head if it wasn't fastened on."

Tommie was glad Granny had kept talking and hadn't expected any answer to her question about the bonnet. The truth was, Tommie hated to wear a bonnet, and she just left it at home whenever she thought she could get away with it.

"When I was a little girl," Granny went on, "bonnets were made with a tiny buttonhole in the top, and whenever a mother put a bonnet on her little girl she'd pull some hair up through that buttonhole and knot a ribbon into it. The knot was big enough so it wouldn't slip back through the buttonhole, and the bonnet had to stay on until the mother was ready for it to be taken off. That's how I learned to wear a bonnet."

Tommie was glad Mamma didn't think bonnets that important.

By this time Granny had her bonnet on and had picked up her berry bucket. As they started up the path that led back to huckleberry ridge, Tommie asked, "What else did you do when you were a little girl, Granny?"

"One thing I had to do was to walk to school with my arms crooked over a broomstick across my back," Granny replied. "That helped me stand and walk straight."

"I'm glad I don't have to do that," said Tommie emphatically.

"You don't need to," Granny observed, "but I had a habit of not standing straight, and my father decided to do something about it. I really hated that broomstick, but it taught me to have good posture."

"Where did your parents come from, Granny?" Tommie asked. She knew, but she never tired of hearing Granny tell the story.

Granny smiled. She didn't mind telling the story again, either. "They grew up on neighboring plantations in the South before the Civil War. Papa's folks had come over from Scotland, and Mamma's folks came from Ireland. When the war broke out, Papa joined the Confederate Army. He was too young to be a regular soldier, so he served as a drummer boy. When the war ended, his home and most of his family were gone, so he came to the Ozarks with an older brother. Later he sent for his sweetheart, and they were married."

"It must have been hard to live on a plantation and have slaves and servants and everything, and then have them taken away," said Tommie thoughtfully.

Clouds covered the sun, and thunder rumbled through the woods.
Granny decided to take the children to the house and out of the storm.

"Yes, I suppose so, but I don't remember either of my parents ever complaining about it," replied Granny.

"Can you sing any of the old songs your mother and daddy taught you?" asked Tommie slyly.

Granny laughed. "So it's a song you've been hinting for! All right, which one?"

"Oh, sing 'Loch Lomond,' please," Tommie requested.

Granny's voice rang out clear and sweet over the hills.

> "By yon bonnie banks and by yon bonnie braes,
> Where the sun shines bright on Loch Lomond,
> Where me and my true love were ever wont to gae,
> On the bonnie, bonnie banks of Loch Lomond.
> Oh, ye tak' the high road and I'll tak' the the low road,
> And I'll be in Scotland afore ye,
> But me and my true love will never meet again
> On the bonnie, bonnie banks of Loch Lomond!"

When Granny finished, Tommie begged, "Will you sing 'Greensleeves' now, Granny? And then the one about the three hunters?"

Granny sang the songs requested, and the mile to the huckleberry patch didn't seem nearly so long as usual. Huckleberry bushes grew all over the ridge and down the hillsides. Great clusters of the purple berries hung from the branches, and soon the plunk of berries dropping in the three buckets was the only sound heard. Tommie and Bud took time to eat all they wanted as they picked.

Not a breeze disturbed the hot air. Little beads of perspiration stood out on the foreheads of the three pickers as the bright sun glared down on them. Granny stood up and glanced at the sky. "Look at that cloud there in the west," she exclaimed. "I think we're going to have a thunderstorm!" Tommie looked up. She didn't like storms of any kind, and that cloud looked black and menacing.

Granny reassured her. "I don't think it will be a bad one. If it starts to rain, we'll stand under those trees over there until it's over. We'll keep pretty dry that way. Let's go ahead and pick our berries."

Tommie kept one eye on the clouds and one eye on the huckleberries as she picked. Soon she heard voices. Looking about she saw Mrs. Pender and her sister talking to Granny. They had come to pick some huckleberries too.

"I don't think we'll stay, though," Mrs. Pender said to Granny. "I don't like that cloud coming up. I think we're going to have a bad storm."

"The children and I are going to stay under those big trees over there if it starts to rain," Granny explained. "We'll be all right."

"I think Alice and I will go on home," Mrs. Pender said. "We can pick huckleberries another day."

Shortly after the other women had gone Granny told Tommie, "Maybe we'd better go back to the house. I left all my windows open, and if it rains all my beds will be soaked. Call Bud and we'll go!"

By this time the cloud covered the sun, and thunder rumbled softly through the hills. Tommie agreed that they should leave the woods. She hadn't been looking forward to standing under those trees when it rained.

About a quarter of a mile from Granny's house Tommie saw Mamma coming to meet them. Mamma cupped her hands to her mouth and called Granny, "Mamma, you and the children had better hurry. It looks like we're going to have a bad storm!"

The first gust of wind whipped Mamma's skirt around her legs, and a sharp crack of thunder emphasized her words. Tommie and Granny and Bud hurried, but the wind blew so strong against them they could hardly reach the house.

When they finally struggled up Granny's back steps, Becky Jane waited just outside the door.

"I was afraid you couldn't get back with all that wind," Becky Jane said to Mamma.

"We made it all right," answered Mamma. She fought to get the door shut, but the wind had it pinned against the side of the house. Granny and Tommie ran to help and between the three of them they managed to pull it closed just as the rain began.

"I've never seen such wind," said Mamma. "I shut the windows before I came out to meet you. It's a good thing—just look at that rain!"

The rain beat down in heavy sheets. The black cloud had grown until now it filled the whole sky. Tree limbs tossed crazily against each other, bending and turning as the wind tore at them. The storm frightened Tommie, but she and Bud stayed at the window.

A loud crash sounded above the roar of the wind. "It's that big chinquapin tree out by your chicken house, Granny," Tommie called. "The wind blew it down!" She jumped back from the window as a flash of lightning cut the room. A crash of thunder followed.

Becky Jane held onto Mamma as hard as she could. Bud and Tommie ran from window to window, peering out as other trees crashed down and limbs tore from trees too sturdy to be blown over. Then a sharp bang from the rear of the house! A hard gust of wind swept in, scattering papers and blowing the tablecloth into the living room.

"The back door," Granny cried. "It must have come unfastened." Mamma, Tommie, and Bud fought the wind and rain for control of the door. When they finally got it shut, Granny slipped the heavy bolt across it.

Tommie turned to Mamma. "Was Daddy out working in the field when you first came down here, Mamma?"

"No," Mamma answered. "He stayed at the house this afternoon to fix something that had broken on the mules' harness."

"I'm glad he did," said Tommie with a sigh of relief.

"You needn't worry about your daddy, Tommie," said her mother gently. "You know he knows more about reading weather signs than anyone else I ever saw. Besides," she added with a grin, "he wouldn't take kindly to you thinking he didn't know enough to come in out of the rain."

Mamma's teasing took away part of Tommie's fear. Anyhow, the wind had died now, and the rain came down softly like an afternoon shower. Within half an hour the storm had passed. Clouds still covered the sky, but the rain stopped.

They stepped outside to see the results of the storm. Several large trees lay uprooted at the edge of the yard, and Tommie picked up fallen tree branches everywhere she walked. The small stream that flowed down the hollow raged over its banks. Tommie and her family would not be able to go home until the water lowered.

Lucinda and her parents came across the road on the other side of the creek and walked to the water's edge. Tommie and Mother went to meet them on their side. Mr. Morris had his arm about his wife's shoulders; her puffy, red eyes told them she had been crying. Lucinda just stood quietly looking at the water.

"Lightning struck our cow and killed her," Mr. Morris called. "We'll have to go ahead and butcher her, but I don't know what we'll do for milk."

"All of us around here have more milk than we can use," Mother told them. "We'll all be glad to share with you until you get another cow."

"I don't know when that'll be." He sighed and turned toward home.

Two hours after the rain stopped the water in the creek subsided enough to let Tommie's family go home. The sun peeked through the clouds now and then, and the moist air carried the sweet fragrance of spring flowers. Dust that had spurted between Tommie's toes earlier in the day had turned to cool, slippery mud.

Daddy looked up as they entered the house. He was still mending the harness. "That was quite a rain we had," he remarked.

"Yes," answered Mamma. "And quite a bit of wind with it!"

Daddy nodded. "I wondered if there might not have been," he said. "I could hear it, but wind never hits here at the house like it does up on the hill. Did it do much damage?"

"A few trees were blown at Mamma's place. And lightning killed the Morrises' cow."

When he returned an hour later he said to Mamma, "It's all taken care of. Mr. Webb had a nice cow he wanted to sell, and the other neighbors said they'd help, so we bought it. We'll take it down to the Morrises in the morning. They've had a hard time getting started here, and they're such nice folks it would be a pity to let them get discouraged and leave."

Several days later Tommie went down to Granny's to borrow a pound of sugar. As Granny poured the sugar into a jar she said, "I went back to the huckleberry patch this morning, Tommie. Do you remember I said we'd wait out the storm under those big trees? Well, that storm blew down every one of those trees."

Tommie gulped. "I guess—we were pretty lucky, weren't we?" she finally managed to say.

"Lucky?" said Granny slowly. "No, not luck, Tommie. Something else, I think. When I was a little girl I used to go to church every week. I wish that you and Bud and the rest of the children could go to church and learn, but—! No, Tommie, it wasn't luck. I think God was watching over us that day!"

For a long time afterward Tommie wondered about a God who took care of people, but she gradually forgot as other things captured her interest.

Spitzie's Practical Joke

Tommie sat under the big white oak tree by the spring. Back and forth, back and forth she shook the jar of cream. When it turned to butter, she would pour the buttermilk into another jar and wash the butter in cold spring water until all the milk was washed out of it, and then she'd mix in a little salt.

Daddy came out and stood by the spring, watching the honeybees that came to get a drink there.

"Are you going to hunt a bee tree, Daddy?" asked Tommie.

"I'm thinking about it," he replied. "I've been watching these bees, and not all of them go off toward Mr. Webb's beehives. Some of them fly off toward the woods when they finish drinking."

That night Daddy took a small box and fitted it with a sliding glass lid. He called it a bee box. The next day he went to town and brought home a small glass bottle labeled "anise oil." Tommie took off the lid and sniffed cautiously. It smelled just like licorice. Tommie didn't like licorice, but Daddy said the bees liked the flavor. Daddy took a few drops of the anise oil and added it to some sugar syrup Mamma had made. Then he dipped a piece of cotton in the syrup and place it in the bee box.

Daddy put the bee box out by the spring and sat down to wait. Before long several bees buzzed inside the box. They eagerly feasted on the syrup. Then Daddy slid the lid shut and captured them all.

One of the bees buzzed up to the top near the glass. Daddy opened the lid and let it out. Up into the air it flew, circled about several times, and then flew toward Mr. Webb's farm. The next bee that Daddy freed flew toward the woods. Daddy took the box and followed in the direction the bee had gone. Then he stopped and let another bee go, following that one farther into the woods. He did that until he had let go all the bees. Then he marked the place where they had led him and came home.

The next morning he caught more bees in his box and went to the spot where he'd left off the evening before. Since some of the bees were from Mr. Webb's hives and went straight home, he had to again mark his place and come home to capture more bees. However, shortly after noon one of the bees he let go flew straight into a hole in a big old oak tree. Daddy went to the tree and watched. Bees were busily coming and going from the hole in the tree. A dull hum told him that here indeed was the bee tree he'd been hunting. He cut a big "X" into the bark of the tree with his pocketknife. That was a sign that the tree was already claimed, in case someone else tracked some of the bees to the tree.

A little later Tommie, waiting, saw her father coming home along the road. "Did you find the bee tree?" she asked.

"Yes, I found it. It's about two miles back in the woods."

"Are you going to cut it today?" asked Bud.

"No, not until tomorrow," Daddy replied.

"May Bud and I go with you when you cut it?" begged Tommie. "We never have seen you cut a bee tree."

"It's a big tree and probably has a lot of honey in it. I could use your help in carrying the honey home," said Daddy.

Early the next morning Daddy gathered old rags and told Bud and Tommie to tie them to the ends of sticks. These, he explained, would be used as torches. Then, taking the torches, an ax, buckets for the honey, and mosquito netting, the group started out. The early morning air felt cool and pleasant.

When they reached the bee tree, Daddy tied the mosquito netting over his head. Then he cleared a circle of brush and leaves down to the soil and rocks and built a fire there. He took his ax and chopped the tree so that it fell uphill. Angry bees swarmed out of the hole in the tree. Daddy called for Tommie to light one of the torches and bring it to him. The smoke would help quiet the bees. When the smoke was thick and the bees less active, he cut a big hole in the tree until he found honey. Tommie brought the buckets, and Daddy filled them. Daddy left the older honey for the bees to take away when they found another hollow tree for a home.

Daddy and Tommie had each been stung by the bees twice, and Bud had been stung once; but they didn't mind because now they had fresh honey.

Carrying the heavy buckets brimming with honey, they started home. They stopped several times to rest. Tommie and Bud broke off bits of the dripping honeycomb and chewed it. Even after the honey was chewed out of it they kept on chewing the wax as if it were chewing gum.

Mamma, delighted with so much honey, poured it in gallon jars and stored them in the big cupboard. The honey would taste good with hot biscuits and the butter Tommie had churned.

The next day Daddy went to town. Before leaving he filled a quart jar with honey and said to Mamma, "I'm going to take this up to Mr. Hermann. I think he'd enjoy it."

"Wait a minute," said Mamma, "and I'll send along a loaf of the bread I made yesterday and some fresh butter. A man living alone as Mr. Hermann does probably gets hungry for such things."

When Daddy drove in from town, the children came out to help carry the groceries.

Daddy said, "Here, Tommie. Mr. Hermann gave me this today. You can have it if you want it; but I don't think it's going to live long." He handed Tommie a thin, shivering brown pup. Daddy continued, "Mr. Hermann said it just came to his place the other morning. He dipped it in some kind of nicotine solution to kill the fleas, and it may kill the dog too. Anyway, see what you can do for it. I'd give it a bath first, if I were you."

Tommie took the little animal into the backyard and put him into a tub of warm, soapy water. Tommie gently worked the warm suds through his matted coat. After soaping and rinsing him several times, she wrapped him in a towel and dried him as best she could. He looked like a different puppy.

She fed him a bowl of milk and then took him into the house to show her parents. She kept him wrapped in the towel as she went into the living room. "See what I have now!" she announced, and uncovered him. In place of the bedraggled little brown creature Daddy had given to Tommie less than an hour before, there stood a perky little pup with a silky snow-white coat!

"Isn't he a beauty?" exulted Tommie. "What kind of dog is he, Daddy?"

"I'd say he's a toy breed of some kind—probably a toy spitz, judging from the way he curls his tail over his back," Daddy replied.

"Then I'll call him Spitzie," Tommie said. "I've never had a dog of my own before."

"What if Bob doesn't like him?" Bud asked.

"I don't know," said Tommie slowly. Up until now Bob had been the only dog on the farm. He had been trained to keep livestock from other farms out of the yard, since farmers could legally let their animals graze along the roadside. He was faithful at his work. Would he know that Spitzie wasn't to be driven away?

But Tommie need not have worried about introducing the two dogs. At first they looked at each other suspiciously. Then Bob nudged Spitzie with his nose. Spitzie reached out a paw and batted Bob's nose. Within minutes they were romping together like the best of friends.

Spitzie became Tommie's shadow, always at her heels. Tommie even wrote a little rhyme about him.

"I have a little doggie
That goes everywhere with me.
The first day that I got him
He was brown as he could be.
I washed him till he was as white
As Mary's little lamb,
And wherever you see Spitzie,
There I am!"

Late one afternoon Tommie and Spitzie went after the cows. Almost full grown now, Spitzie still reached only halfway to Tommie's knee. He ran all over the pasture investigating various sights and smells, but he always stayed in sight of Tommie.

Now and then Tommie stopped and listened for the sound of the bell Daddy had tied around Lassie's neck. She heard nothing. Tommie hunted and hunted, and finally found the cows standing quietly in the woods with Lassie lying nearby. But no bell hung from Lassie's neck. She had lost it.

When Tommie came in late with the cows, she told Daddy about the missing cowbell, and that night he put another bell around Lassie's neck.

Not long afterward Daddy found the lost bell as he was going through the pasture. The rope was frayed and had broken. He hung the bell on a limb of the peach tree near the front door.

Late that afternoon, Spitzie saw the frayed rope hanging from the bell in the tree. He gave it a tug, and the bell clanged. The noise of the bell awoke Bob from his nap in the shade of the house. Bells meant livestock, and his responsibility was to keep them away from the house. Barking loudly, he dashed to the gate to drive the intruders away, but none were there. Spitzie watched Bob with interest. After running about the yard a while, Bob went back to his place in the shade.

This performance amused Tommie, who sat laughing on the front steps. "What will Spitzie think of next?" she called to Mamma who was inside watching through the open door.

As soon as Bob went back to sleep Spitzie trotted quietly up to the rope and gave it another tug, and then stood back to watch the excitement. Bob started up again and ran barking to the gate. When he found no animals there, he carefully explored the whole yard and then lay down to sleep again.

Tommie turned to Mamma and asked, "Shall I put the rope up out of Spitzie's reach? You can see he's just doing that for fun. He seems to know Bob will jump up when he hears that bell. I feel sorry for poor Bob."

Mamma thought a moment. "Let's leave the bell where it is," she suggested, "and see how long Bob takes to realize that a trick has been played on him."

Twice more, as Tommie watched, Spitzie tugged the bell rope and sent Bob racing to drive away cows that weren't there. The next time, though, Bob got up, looked around, and settled himself right back in his place. After that the sound of the bell never even aroused him from his rest.

"Mamma," said Tommie anxiously, "do you think Bob will ever chase the livestock away from the yard again? He doesn't even seem to hear the bell now."

"I think he will," said Mamma. "He's just learned the sound of this particular bell and knows it doesn't have a cow attached to it."

A few days later Mamma's theory proved true. Several of Mr. Pender's cows wandered up the road, and Bob, hearing their bells, came charging to keep them out of the yard. Spitzie, too, came running and barking.

"Why, Spitzie," exclaimed Tommie, "have you decided to help Bob instead of annoying him? You'll turn out to be a proper farm dog yet."

Spitzie licked her hand and then went to join Bob in the shade of the house to take a nap.

Tommie decided to use twice as much of the freckle cream as the label said to. She spread a thick layer of the cream on her face and neck.

Beauty in a Jar

"Oh, dear," Tommie mourned as she faced herself in the mirror. "I get more freckles every year. They don't fade away in the winter, but in the summer they increase until there's hardly any space left between them. Pretty soon I will be just one big freckle. I hate them!"

All that day, Tommie could not forget her problem. At supper she mentioned it to Mamma.

"Mamma, I'm just plain sick and tired of these freckles," she complained. "Isn't there anything we can do to get rid of them?"

"Well," answered her mother, "you know how we tease you every year in tomato time because tomato juice fades the freckles around your mouth and leaves a pale ring there. Why don't you try putting tomato juice all over your face?"

"I did try that once for several days. I put tomato juice on my face, and when it dried it felt awful!" said Tommie.

"Even worse than freckles?" queried her brother Bud.

"Every bit as bad," declared Tommie, "and it didn't take away the freckles, either."

"What else have you tried?" asked Mamma.

"Well, once I tried a pack of buttermilk and oatmeal, but it made my face so stiff I could hardly move a muscle!"

"I remember that," laughed Bud. "You really looked funny!"

"You wouldn't think it was funny if you had freckles!" snapped Tommie.

"I do have freckles," Bud pointed out.

"Well, not nearly as many as I do," argued Tommie. "Besides, you're a boy, and freckles don't make any difference to a—"

"Tommie! Bud!" interrupted their father. "Stop this bickering at once or you'll have to leave the table. I want no more discussion about freckles, do you hear?"

Tommie and Bud ate the rest of the meal in silence.

Several days later Daddy returned from town and handed Tommie a small box. "Now, here, Tommie," he said. "Here's something that may make you feel better about those freckles you've been complaining of so much."

Tommie opened the box quickly. Inside was a small jar labeled "Freckle Cream." The directions read, "Apply a thin layer of freckle cream to skin at bedtime. In the morning wash off with Freckle Cream Soap. Wear a hat when outside. If these directions are followed faithfully for six weeks, marked improvement will be noted."

"Oh, how wonderful," cried Tommie. "Thank you, Daddy!"

"School starts in three weeks," thought Tommie to herself. "If I use twice as much of that freckle cream on my face, maybe I can get rid of my freckles before school starts. Just think! Won't everyone be surprised when I come to school without freckles. They'll have to quit calling me 'Freckles' and 'Tiger Lily' and 'Spots.' Oh, I can hardly wait!"

That night Tommie spread a thick layer of the cream on her face and neck. It smelled good and felt much nicer than the tomato juice and buttermilk treatments she had tried before. She wished she had enough cream to put on her arms, too, but that would have to wait until she could get another jar.

The next morning Tommie read again the directions on the jar. "Wash off with Freckle Cream Soap." But Daddy had not bought any Freckle Cream Soap. Then Tommie thought, "If I keep washing that cream off, how is it going to take the freckles off in three weeks? I'll just leave it on and it can work twice as long!"

"Tommie! Bud! Come on, we're going to pick tomatoes today," Daddy called.

As Tommie started out the door, Mamma stopped her. "Here's your bonnet, Tommie," she said. "Aren't you supposed to wear something on your head when you're using that freckle cream?"

"Yes, Mamma," answered Tommie.

"Well, remember to keep this on," said Mamma. "You know you have a habit of taking it off fifteen minutes after you get outside!"

"All right, Mamma," said Tommie as she took the bonnet and ran to catch up with Daddy.

Tommie really meant to wear the bonnet even though she didn't like it. It was an old-fashioned creation of blue calico with strips of cardboard inserted between layers of the cloth so the brim stood out stiffly from her face. Granny had made it for her at the beginning of the summer. Tommie tied the strings under her chin, picked up a bushel basket, and began picking tomatoes with the others.

The hot August sun sent perspiration streaming down her face. Without thinking, Tommie took off the bonnet, wiped her face, and went on with her work. The bonnet spent the rest of the morning on top of a stump.

The sun climbed higher in the sky and beat down hotter. Tommie's face began to sting. "It's probably just that freckle cream working," she said to herself. But the stinging grew worse. By the time Daddy said it was time to go to the house for dinner, Tommie's face was burning so badly she could hardly keep back the tears.

"Oh, Tommie!" gasped Mamma as the girl entered the house. "Whatever has happened to your face?"

"I don't know, " mumbled Tommie, "but it hurts terribly. It must be that freckle cream I put on it!"

"Did you follow the directions and only put a little bit on last night?" asked Mamma.

"Well—no—I—I put on a little more than it said to," replied Tommie. "I wanted to get rid of all my freckles before school started."

"And did you wash it off this morning?"

"No, I thought—I thought I'd let it work a little longer," Tommie explained lamely.

"And it's plain to see you took your bonnet off right after you started to work," Mamma persisted. "Well, talking won't help matters now. Come on and get into bed and I'll put some sweet cream on your face. You won't be able to go to the field this afternoon, probably not for several days. That's one of the worst sunburns I've ever seen."

"You see, Tommie," said Mamma as she sat on Tommie's bed to renew the cream-soaked cloths, "that freckle cream contained bleaching chemicals. The directions are there to prevent just such accidents as this."

"I know, I know, Mamma," moaned Tommie. "I'll always follow directions carefully after this, really I will."

"Tommie, dear, the problem is deeper than that," Mamma went on. "You've been too concerned about those freckles, about how you look."

"But, Mamma," protested Tommie, "every girl wants to be pretty."

"Of course," said Mamma, "but real beauty doesn't come out of a jar. It comes from inside, from the heart and mind. If you have beauty inside, it will shine out in your face, in everything you do or say, and people won't notice your freckles at all. Will you try to remember that?"

"I'll try, at least," said Tommie soberly.

Tommie's Painful Lesson

Daddy took the catalog down from the shelf. "School will begin in a couple of weeks," he said, "so we'd better get an order off for whatever the children need."

"Bud needs overalls and shirts. Tommie needs shoes , and she and Becky Jane need material for school dresses," replied Mamma.

Tommie reached over and ruffled Becky Jane's curls. "So you are going to school with me this year," she said.

Becky Jane nodded, her big eyes solemn. "Do you like school, Sissy?"

"Oh, yes, I love school," exclaimed Tommie, forgetting how eager she felt each spring for school to end. "You'll love school too. Come on, let's see if Mamma will let us pick out our own dress material."

"I think each of you will need three new dresses," Mamma said. "I'll let you pick out material for two of them, and I'll pick out the other."

Two heads, one with dark pigtails and the other with blond curls, bent over the catalog, intent on the pictures of cotton prints.

"I know!" exclaimed Tommie. "Let's get one piece of material and both of us have a dress made from it. You know—sister dresses, Becky Jane!"

Becky Jane's eyes shone. "Oh, goody," she said. "What color shall we get?"

"What about blue?" suggested Tommie. "We both look nice in blue." Soon they agreed on a soft blue with tiny yellow flowers.

Then Becky Jane picked out a pink gingham, and Tommie chose a green plaid. Mamma wrote down their choices.

"Which are you picking for me, Mamma?" Tommie asked.

"That's going to be a secret," replied Mamma. "You'll have to wait and see. I will tell you this—I'm going to try something different this year for you, Tommie!"

"Oh, Mamma, tell me, please, please!" begged Tommie.

"No," said Mamma. "You can wait a week until the order gets here!"

"A whole week," wailed Tommie. "That's practically forever!"

"Tommie!" her father spoke sharply. "Stop complaining and come over here. I want to measure your feet for shoes."

Tommie went over to her father's chair. "Now," he directed, "put your right foot down here on this paper and stand still while I draw around it."

Tommie knew the shoes would be the same as always—plain brown oxfords, not particularly pretty but sturdy enough to last a year.

The order was finished and mailed the next day. Tommie sighed. A week was such a long time to wait. She didn't have much time to brood about it, though. Right after breakfast Daddy drove up to the yard with the wagon.

"Come on, Tommie, Bud! We're going to Mr. Hermann's for apples this morning," he called.

Tommie and Bud climbed eagerly into the wagon. They loved to visit Mr. Hermann. He could tell fascinating stories about things he had done as a fireman in a big city, a prospector in Alaska, and a farmer on the west coast. Today, however, they were all too busy for stories. Tommie and Bud picked up apples from the ground and put them in baskets. Daddy climbed the trees and picked from there. Mr. Hermann took the apples Tommie and Bud picked up and pressed out the juice in a cider mill. By noon they had picked all the apples Daddy thought they needed. Daddy paid Mr. Hermann for them and for the two big cans of apple juice, and they hurried home.

Mamma poured part of the apple juice into a big gallon jar and told Tommie to set it in the cold spring water to cool for dinner.

After the meal, Mamma said, "We're going to make apple butter this afternoon. Bud, you bring the big iron kettle and set it out by the spring. Then gather some wood for the fire. Tommie, you and I will peel the apples, and we'll have to hurry. It takes a long time for apple butter to cook."

Mamma and Tommie sat in the cool shade of the big white oak tree and peeled apples. It didn't seem long until the kettle was full of the peeled, quartered apples. Bud had a good fire going by this time and they placed the kettle over it. Mamma poured some of the apple juice into the kettle over the apples and said, "Now, Tommie, you stir this once in a while, and I'll check on it now and then myself."

After the apples had cooked into mushy applesauce, Mamma added sugar and spices. "You'll have to stir more often now, Tommie," she said. "The thicker this gets the more likely it is to burn. Bud, you take care of the fire. Keep the fire to one side and push the red-hot coals under the kettle."

Tommie stirred, and stirred, and stirred. The mixture grew darker and fragrant with spices. Thick bubbles came to the surface and broke with a "plop," sending up puffs of steam like miniature volcanoes. Once in a while Bud would take the wooden paddle and stir for a few minutes so Tommie could rest. Finally Mamma decided the apple butter had cooked long enough. Tommie gave her the paddle with a sigh of relief, and she and Bud took the kettle from the fire.

Mamma rinsed and scalded the glass jars and lids and poured in the apple butter. When she finished she looked at the filled jars with pride. "I think one more kettleful will be enough," she said. "We'll do that tomorrow morning."

After finishing the apple butter next morning, Bud and Tommie carried the jars to the cellar Daddy had dug into the hillside. Jars of peas and green beans Mamma had put up in the spring, the huckleberries and blackberries that came in early summer, and the tomatoes and tomato juice they had canned two weeks before sat in gleaming rows on the shelves.

"There's not much danger of our starving this winter," Bud laughed.

"Doesn't seem so," Tommie agreed.

The next two days Tommie and Mamma made applesauce. Applesauce didn't tire Tommie like apple butter, because it didn't have to be stirred for hours. One day Tommie chopped cabbage for sauerkraut, and another day she and Mamma canned peaches. Almost before she knew it, the week ended and the mail carrier had left a huge parcel at the mailbox.

The children jumped up and down in excitement as Mamma opened the package. Tommie and Becky Jane fingered the soft blue for their "sister dresses," the pink gingham, and the green plaid. For Becky Jane's other dress Mamma had picked a plain yellow, but for Tommie she had chosen black with large patches of vivid tulips in yellow, pink, red, and white. It was beautiful—but black! None of the girls Tommie knew ever wore black! She didn't know what to say.

Mother smiled understandingly. "Never mind, Tommie. When I get the dress made I think you'll like it. We'll do that one first—we'll start it tomorrow."

The next morning Mamma cut a pattern from a newspaper. She fitted the pattern to Tommie, then she cut and sewed the material. Tommie cooked dinner and did the housework so Mamma would have more time to sew. By noon the next day the dress was finished. Mamma had it princess style, fitted to the waist and flaring softly into the skirt. It had short sleeves and a round, collarless neckline. Tommie thought it looked beautiful. Even Daddy admired it when he came in at noon.

Tommie looked at the dress and wondered who but Mamma would have seen such possibilities in that piece of black print. Who else would have had the courage to try something so new and different for a girl Tommie's age?

After dinner Daddy said to Mamma, "I'm going to take a look around through the woods this afternoon. We'll want to get some walnuts and hickory nuts later on, and I'll see how the wild grapes are doing. Tommie and Bud have worked hard this week, so they may come along if they like!"

"I want to go too," cried Becky Jane.

"You're too little, Becky Jane," Daddy explained. "We're going to walk a long way!" The comers of Becky Jane's mouth turned down. Tears welled in her blue eyes.

"Why, Becky Jane, I need you here," Mamma said hastily. "I want to start your pink dress this afternoon, and you'll have to be here for me to fit it!"

"Really, Mamma? All right then, I'll stay." The corners of Becky Jane's mouth curved up again in a delighted smile. Tommie let out a breath of relief. The walk would have been no fun if Becky Jane had been left home crying.

"May I wear my new shoes, Mamma?" Tommie asked, "It will be much easier to walk if I wear shoes."

"You'd better wear your old shoes, Tommie," answered Mamma. "Sometimes new shoes pinch until they are broken in."

"My new shoes fit fine," insisted Tommie. "I've already tried them on. This walk would be a good time to break them in."

"But, Tommie, sometimes new shoes feel fine when you first put them on, but they start hurting after you've worn them a little while."

"These won't," said Tommie. "Please let me wear them."

"But—" began Mamma when Daddy interrupted her to say, "Let Tommie wear her new shoes if she wants to. Perhaps it will be good for her."

Something in his voice as he said this made Tommie look at him, but he said nothing more. She ran and put her new shoes on over clean white socks and was ready to go.

Tommie and Bud followed Daddy across the pasture until they came to a set of wagon tracks winding across the woods. This was known as the "ridge road," and it led about three miles back to a valley whose sides were pitted with caves. A creek bed, usually dry, wandered through the valley, and on each side of it walnut trees grew in abundance. Most years the walnut trees bore great quantities of nuts, and one day was set aside each fall for gathering them.

As they walked Tommie began to feel an uncomfortable rubbing of her left heel. Shortly afterward the right one felt the same. She wiggled her feet into the shoes as far toward the toes as possible, but before long her feet had worked into the old uncomfortable position again. She thought with dismay of the miles ahead before they came to the valley—and of the long walk home.

Once when Daddy stopped to show them some plants that they would gather later for medicine Tommie sneaked a look at her heels. Large blisters had formed on each one. Maybe it would be better to go without her shoes, she thought, so she took them off, tied the strings together, and hung them around her neck. She was able to keep up with Daddy and Bud as they walked down the ridge road, for the wagon tracks were fairly smooth; but she fell behind when they started across the woods to look for wild grapes.

"Tommie," called her father, "you're going to have to keep up with us. Can't you walk faster?"

"Yes, Daddy, I'm coming," Tommie answered. She quickly slipped the shoes on again. Hobbling painfully, she managed to keep up for a while, then she lagged behind again as her feet began to hurt worse.

"Tommie, are those shoes hurting your feet?" Daddy demanded.

"Yes," Tommie admitted. "They have worn blisters on both my heels."

"I thought you said you had tried them on and they fit fine," he reminded her.

"I did say that," replied Tommie. "I guess I just didn't wear them long enough to find out."

"But you insisted on wearing them, didn't you? Your mother tried to tell you this might happen, remember?"

"I remember," Tommie said, banging her head. "I know I should have listened when you and Mamma tried to tell me."

By this time the blisters had broken and left brown bloodstains on her socks. Daddy shook his head and sighed. "I thought something like this might happen. I hope you learn a lesson from it, Tommie, so you will not always insist on having your own way, or feel that you know more than your parents."

"It's a pretty painful lesson, Daddy, but I guess that's the kind that I'm not likely to forget in a hurry," Tommie said.

"See that you don't forget, Tommie," said Daddy. "Now, you'll have to go on home. We are only about a quarter of a mile from the main road, so go over this hill and down the hollow. You'll come out about where the creek crosses the road by Mr. Pender's fence. From there on you won't have any trouble. Go along, now."

Tommie had to put the shoes on again because the ground was too rough to go barefoot. It seemed hours before she finally reached the main road, for her bleeding feet hurt worse with every step.

When she reached the road she took off her shoes and was able to walk much faster.

Mamma had seen her coming and met her at the door. "Why are you back so soon, Tommie?" she asked.

"My new shoes rubbed blisters on my heels," Tommie confessed.

Mamma looked at Tommie's feet. "I'll say they did," she exclaimed in dismay. "Oh, Tommie, when will you ever learn?"

"I already have learned, Mamma. I had nothing else to think about all the way home," Tommie answered.

Mamma brought warm water from the stove, and Tommie soaked her feet for a long time. How comforting the warm water was to her sore heels! Then Mamma applied vaseline and clean white bandages. "There, now," she said. "That should feel better."

"Oh, yes, it does. Thank you, Mamma."

When school started the next week Tommie was not able to wear her new black dress and new oxfords as she had planned. She wore the dress, which everyone admired, but it didn't look nearly so pretty with last year's old scuffed shoes. And even last year's old shoes hurt Tommie's sore feet, but she didn't complain. She knew she deserved her punishment.

Molasses in a Shoe

The summer dragged on, hot and dry. Day after day farmers looked into the skies, hoping for signs of rain to save their parched crops. Many springs and wells in the area ran dry, and some of the neighbors began to bring big milk cans and fill them from the spring at Tommie's house. That spring never went dry.

One morning Tommie, Bud, and Daddy climbed up the hill to the field beside the pasture. Rows of watermelons that Daddy had planted lay ripening in the hot sun. In spite of the heat and dry air watermelons tasted sweet and good. Every day Daddy put some of the melons in the spring by the house to get cold. When the neighbors came to fill their water cans, he treated them to thick slices of cold, sweet melon.

Daddy moved about the patch selecting the ripe melons.

"Now listen, Tommie, and you too, Bud, and I'll show you how to tell a ripe watermelon from a green one." He thumped the melon beside him with his thumb and forefinger. "See," he said, "this one is green—it sounds hollow. A ripe one sounds like this," and he thumped the toe of his shoe. That made a dull, solid sound.

Tommie thought she could tell the difference, so she thumped several melons, trying to decide the ripe ones from the green ones. Finally Daddy said, "I think you have the idea now, Tommie. Try picking out a ripe one and we'll cut it to eat here."

Tommie ran up and down a row thumping melon after melon.

She chose one and brought it to Daddy. He opened his pocket knife and jabbed it into the melon. The melon split halfway down its length, a sure sign of a just-right melon. Tommie beamed with delight. Daddy cut generous slices, and the three sat eating them.

Tommie looked into the distance, hoping to see rainclouds somewhere along the horizon, but found none. As she looked, her father's voice, softly, hardly above a whisper, called, "Tommie! Tommie! Look here!"

Tommie looked. A tiny ruby-throated hummingbird hovered by her father. Then he thrust his long, slender bill into the red meat of the melon slice that Daddy held. The bird's iridescent green back glittered in the sunshine. He backed away to remove his bill from the watermelon and then darted away in humming flight.

"Hunger and thirst made him desperate enough to trust man," Daddy said. "Who knows how many other birds and animals out in the woods are suffering from hunger and thirst?"

Daddy took half the watermelon and crushed the center pulp into juicy slush. Placing it a dozen feet away, he sat down and motioned for Tommie and Bud to be still and watch. Within minutes six hummingbirds hovered over the melon, drinking its sweet juice.

Every day after that Daddy opened a watermelon for the hummingbirds. At times it seemed to Tommie that the tiny little creatures filled the air with their flashing emerald green and ruby red. They showed no fear of Daddy, Tommie, and Bud, who sat nearby to watch.

Days marched on, and still the rain didn't come.

One afternoon after dinner, Mamma said to Tommie, "I want to go down and help Granny finish that quilt she has pieced. Do you think you can take care of things here at the house?"

"Of course, Mamma," Tommie said.

"I won't be back until about five o'clock," Mamma went on. "It would be a great help if you'd start supper for me."

A tiny ruby-throated hummingbird hovered by Daddy. Then he thrust his slender bill into the red meat of the melon slice Daddy was holding.

"All right, Mamma," said Tommie, secretly delighted at the thought of having the whole kitchen to herself.

" I'll take Becky Jane with me," said Mamma, "and that will make it easier for you."

After Mamma and Becky Jane left, Tommie sat for a few minutes and thought about supper. What should she cook? Bread, of course, and potatoes. She'd pick some green beans and cook them too. For a salad she decided on lettuce and tomatoes, and she'd make a cake for dessert, Of course it was much too early to start supper. She had the whole long, idle afternoon before her, and that was so unusual she hardly knew how to use it.

Before Tommie had time to make any plans, Bud and his friend Paul came in from the pasture where they had picked a small bucket of blackberries. Tommie took the berries into the kitchen, and the boys followed. Bud took his rubber ball from his pocket. "Here, Paul, catch," he called.

Paul caught the ball, but his throw back went wild and the ball lodged on top of the kitchen cupboard.

"Wait a minute. I'll get it," said Bud, and he climbed easily onto the top of the bucket of molasses that Mamma kept beside the cupboard. Bud had no sooner gotten his weight onto the bucket than the lid folded and one foot sank into the molasses!

All three children stared aghast! Then Bud slowly lifted his foot out of the bucket and stood as the sticky molasses ran down into a puddle on the floor. What a mess! Fortunately the bucket was not full; but Bud's shoe was full of molasses, and one overall leg was soaked almost halfway to his knee.

Finally Tommie found her voice. "You'll have to take off those overalls, Bud," she said. "I'll wash them, and you can clean your shoe."

Bud changed overalls and then filled the washboiler with water from the spring. While he built a fire outside to heat the wash water, Tommie took warm water from the reservoir of the stove to wash the molasses off the kitchen floor. "Oh, well," she said to herself, "as long as I'm about it, I may as well just scrub the whole kitchen floor."

When the kitchen floor sparkled clean, Tommie went out beside the spring where Bud had the wash water heating. Tommie dipped some of it into the washtub that sat on a bench nearby. Then she got the big bar of strong laundry soap from the kitchen and shaved bits of it into the warm water.

"It's a pity to waste all this nice soapy hot water on just one pair of overalls," she thought. "I may as well do the rest of the washing too." She sorted the clothes and put them in neat piles on the ground beside the bench. Taking the scrubboard, she began to wash. She rubbed and scrubbed, and then rinsed; first the white clothes, then the colored ones, then the towels, and last the overalls. She left the sheets, for they were too big for her to handle.

Just as she was finishing the overalls, Mr. Hermann drove into the yard with two big cans in his buggy. He had come for water.

"Well, Tommie," he remarked, "I see you've started doing the family wash. You're a mite young for that, aren't you?"

"I don't usually do it," explained Tommie, "but Bud needed a pair of his overalls washed—"

"He fell in the molasses," interrupted Paul, eager to tell part of the story.

Mr. Hermann threw back his head and laughed. "So you fell in the molasses, did you, Bud?"

Bud nodded sheepishly.

"Did I ever tell you about the time—" Mr. Hermann began. Tommie, Bud, and Paul sat up eagerly. This was how Mr. Hermann usually began his stories.

"Oh, please tell us," they begged.

"Well," said Mr. Hermann, "when I worked for the Baltimore fire department many years ago, we were sitting around playing checkers one afternoon when an alarm came in. We harnessed the horses to the big red engine in no time at all and went thundering through the streets with the bell clanging and dogs barking."

The children had never seen a fire engine, except in pictures, but Mr. Hermann's stories made everything so real that they felt as if they rode on the engine with him.

"When we arrived at the fire, we found a pickle factory in flames. The fire seemed to have started in the storage room where supplies were kept. One of our men, seeing one of the rafters flaming, climbed up onto a huge barrel of mustard to play the hose on the burning wood. He didn't notice that the top of the barrel was weakened and charred from the fire. It gave way with him and dumped him in mustard up to his armpits."

The children laughed heartily as they imagined the scene, and Mr. Hermann smiled at their amusement. "That was a mighty disgusted man, you can just guess," he went on. "And he didn't have a sister there to wash his clothes for him, either, Bud. He had to wash them himself when we got back to the station. Forever after that, as long as he worked with us, everyone called him Mustard."

He took out his watch. "'Why, here it is nearly four o'clock," he exclaimed. "I'd better get my water cans filled and hurry home."

"Four o'clock!" repeated Tommie. "I'd better hurry and start supper." She ran into the house while Bud and Paul stayed outside to help Mr. Hermann fill his water cans.

"Now, let me see," she said to herself, "I'll pick the beans first and since I'm in a hurry I'll cook the potatoes with the jackets on."

When the vegetables were cooking, Tommie got ready to make the cake. There was no cookbook in the house—Mamma didn't need one—but Tommie was sure she could make a cake. She sifted and measured and combined and stirred. Finally she poured the batter into a big pan and placed it in the oven. Then she hurried to the garden for lettuce and tomatoes. The lettuce was strong tasting and tough from lack of rain, and the tomatoes were small, but when she finished the salad., Tommie decided it tasted pretty good.

She set the table and made gravy to put on the potatoes. It was a little lumpy, but she beat it with the eggbeater and it looked better. Then she took another peek at the cake. The top bubbled more like pudding than cake, and the batter hadn't risen one bit. "I'll let it bake a little while longer," she said to herself, but she felt it would take more than just a longer baking time to turn it into a real cake.

Fifteen minutes later she removed the cake from the oven. It still looked more like pudding than cake. She let it cool a bit, then took a spoonful and nibbled at it cautiously. "Why, this is good," she said in surprise. "It isn't cake, but it's good. I'll set it out on the bench by the spring to cool. Mamma will be here pretty soon, and I want to have supper all ready by the time she comes in."

That done, Tommie sat down to rest for a moment. It seemed the first time she'd been able to relax since Mamma had left after dinner. Before long Paul came running in. "Tommie, Tommie—did you put some food in a pan on the bench out by the spring? Well, Bud's dog ate it!"

Tommie held her head in her hands for a moment, then got up wearily. "I guess the only thing to do," she muttered, "is to have those blackberries the boys brought in. I'll pick them over, and put sugar on them and serve them with cream for dessert."

She had finished putting them in bowls and was sprinkling them with sugar when Mamma came in.

"As I came up the road, Tommie, I saw the washing on the line," Mamma said. "You didn't have to do that." Then she noticed the kitchen floor. "And you scrubbed the kitchen too. But, Tommie, I wanted you to have this afternoon just for yourself. You didn't have to do all this work!"

Tommie's smile looked a little tired. "Just let me tell you all that happened, Mamma!"

When she had finished, Mamma said, "You took your responsibilities seriously, Tommie, and I'm proud of you. Now I think you deserve a rest. I'll send Bud after the cows, and you won't have to help with the milking."

"I am tired," admitted Tommie. "But I'm glad you think I did well this afternoon."

"You're beginning to grow up, Tommie," said Mamma. "Being able to take responsibility is one of the signs."

Tommie went to bed early. As she slept, dark clouds came out of the west and covered the moon. That night it rained.

Sunday School on Saturday

"Mamma, there's a strange dog out here in the yard," said Tommie. "He must have gotten lost in the rain last night."

Mamma came to the door. A big, beautiful collie came up to the steps and stood, slowly wagging his tail.

"Mamma, may I keep him?" Tommie begged. "I get so lonesome without a dog of my own."

Spitzie had disappeared several months earlier, and a neighbor had since told Tommie that he had been taken in by a family some miles away. Tommie didn't know why he had run away, but since her neighbor said the children of the new family adored him, Tommie hadn't the heart to ask for him back. Bud's dog, Bob, had recently died of old age. For several weeks there had been no dog at all on the farm. And now this beautiful collie came trotting up and didn't seem to have an owner.

"Why, Tommie, I don't know if you can keep him or not," said Mamma. "A dog like that is pretty sure to belong to someone. We'll have Daddy see if he can find out where this dog belongs."

"Well, I'm going to feed him," Tommie declared, "so if he does not belong anywhere he will want to stay here!"

She put a big bowl of dog food out for the collie and stroked his silky coat as he ate. When he finished his food, he lay down in the shade of the house in Bob's old place and went to sleep as if he'd always lived on the farm.

Tommie knew Daddy wouldn't go to town for another several days, so the owner couldn't possibly be found until then. Meanwhile she would pretend the dog belonged to her.

Right from the start he seemed to take Spitzie's place at Tommie's heels, going with her after the cows and in every doggy way showing his affection for her. Tommie called him Collie, and he answered to the name from the first day.

About three days later Uncle Bill came by for a visit and noticed Collie.

"Well, well," he said, patting Collie on the head, "how did you get here? Aren't you a long way from home?"

Tommie's heart sank. "Oh, Uncle Bill, does he belong to someone? Do you know whose he is?"

"Oh, no, he doesn't belong to anyone in particular," Uncle Bill said. "Old Collie, here, has just sort of been the town dog in Ridgeway for years, and I wondered how he got so far from home."

"I don't know how he got here," said Tommie. "He Just appeared in the yard one day. Do you suppose anyone will mind if I keep him?"

"I don't see any reason why you can't keep him," said Uncle Bill. "The people in Ridgeway will probably be glad for him to have a good home and someone to feed him regularly."

"Then he's my dog from now on!" said Tommie happily. "And did you say his name is Collie?"

"That's what people in Ridgeway called him," answered her uncle.

"That's what I've been calling him too," said Tommie. "No wonder he comes when I call him. I've been using his real name."

As the summer grew hotter, Collie seemed to suffer from the heat. One day Tommie decided that his long, heavy coat was too much for any dog to have to wear in such hot weather. Taking the scissors from Mamma's sewing box, she called Collie to her. He sat trustingly as she clipped away at his coat. Some streak of mischief in Tommie made her decide to leave the ruff of fur around his neck so he would resemble a lion.

"Now," she said to him when she was finished, "you will be cooler. Doesn't that feel better already?"

But Collie only whimpered and he slunk away to hide under the back porch. When it was time to go for the cows, Tommie called him, but he wouldn't come. He only looked at her darkly from his hiding place, and she had to go without him.

When she came in with the cows Daddy asked, "Where's Collie?"

"He's under the porch and he won't come out," Tommie answered.

"Is he sick?" Daddy inquired. "Maybe a snake bit him."

"No, he isn't sick," said Tommie. "I clipped off some of his hair so he'd be cooler, and he went and hid under the porch."

Daddy bent down and looked under the porch.

"Why, Tommie!" said Daddy in exasperation. "What a thing to do! Think how you'd feel if we cut your hair and just left a strip on top like a—a Mohawk Indian. Wouldn't you hide too?"

"I guess I would," answered Tommie.

"On a farm you have to learn to be kind to your animals, Tommie; you know that," Daddy continued.

"But, Daddy, I didn't hurt him," protested Tommie.

"You made him look odd, and he feels ashamed," said Daddy "That's being unkind. It may be some time before Collie learns to trust you again."

"I'm sorry," said Tommie. "I'll try to get him to trust me again. I didn't mean to be unkind to him. I just thought that he'd be cooler if some of his hair was off!"

"Next time you have an idea like that you'd better ask your mother or me first," Daddy said.

For the next two weeks Collie stayed under the porch most of the time. Tommie took his food to him there, talked to him, petted him, and did everything she knew to let him know how sorry she felt. Finally one day he walked from under the porch and trotted at her heels as she went for the cows. Tommie knew she'd been forgiven.

If she hadn't been so concerned about Collie, Tommie would have noticed that Daddy was writing and receiving an unusual number of letters in the mail. One day as he and Mamma were reading and discussing one of them, Tommie came in. Later she asked Mamma what was happening.

"Well," said Mamma, "in a couple of weeks Daddy's parents are going to celebrate their golden wedding anniversary. They are going to have a big party!"

"A party!" exclaimed Tommie. "Are we going?"

"Yes, we are," answered Mamma. "And nearly all of Daddy's sisters and brothers are going to be there too. It will be quite a family reunion."

"Do I know any of these aunts and uncles?" asked Tommie.

"You probably remember Aunt Nola, but I don't think you'll know any of the rest of them."

"Will there be anyone my age at the party?"

"Your Aunt Marty has a boy, Val, just older than you, and a girl, Delores, a year younger. Uncle Rollie has a boy about your age and one Bud's age. Uncle Al has a baby girl. The rest of your uncles and aunts have no children."

"I think it will be fun to get acquainted with cousins I've never met before," said Tommie. "I wish they lived closer so we could see them more often."

"It would be nice," agreed Mamma. "Daddy's family is scattered through several states. I've always felt fortunate that my family stayed together in this area."

Mamma ordered material and made new dresses for Tommie and Becky Jane to wear to the reunion. Tommie's was green, her favorite color, and Becky Jane had blue.

The night before they left home, Mamma brought in two washtubs and filled one with water. She placed the empty one on the kitchen floor and put the other on the stove to warm the water. Then each one took a bath.

When Tommie finished with her bath and got ready for bed, Mamma called her. "Come here, Tommie—I'm going to put your hair up in rags and see if we can't get some curl into it."

Lock by lock Mamma knotted strips of rags into Tommie's long, dark, straight hair, still damp from her bath. Tommie had never had it done before and she didn't like it. She had to laugh at herself, though, when she saw herself in the mirror. Knots of rag stuck up all over her head.

When she went to bed, the knots dug into her head; and this discomfort, combined with the excitement of what the next day promised, caused her a restless night.

All the family got up earlier than usual the next morning. As soon as they finished chores and breakfast, they changed into their good clothes. Mamma brushed Becky Jane's curls and took the rag curlers out of Tommie's hair. Then she brushed it.

"Oh, Mamma!" wailed Tommie when she looked in the mirror. "It looks just like a brush pile!"

"It didn't curl the way I'd hoped it would," Mamma admitted.

"Can't I put some water on it to smooth it, and then just braid it the way I usually do?" Tommie asked. "I wasn't born with curly hair like Becky Jane, so I might just as well be myself!"

"You're right, Tommie," said Mamma. "Go ahead and fix your braids."

By eight o'clock everyone was ready, and an uncle with a car came for them. Grandpa's house was about twenty-five miles away. When they got there, a swarm of relatives immediately surrounded them. Aunt Nola came and took Tommie's hand. "Come over and meet your cousins," she said. "Here is Bob, Gene, Val, and Delores. This is Tommie," she said to the others.

The boys went back to their game. Tommie said to Delores, "I haven't been to Grandma's house since I was just a little girl. After I go say Hello to Grandma and Grandpa I want to look around a bit. Do you want to come with me?"

"Yes," answered Delores. "We got here last night, and everyone has been so busy this morning I haven't had a chance to see much."

When Tommie went to speak to her grandparents, Grandpa reached out and gave one of her braids a gentle pull. "When I was a boy all girls wore braids," he said. "Tell me, Tommie—do you still like to sing? When you were a little girl you sang all the time!"

"Yes, I still like to sing," Tommie answered.

"Will you sing me a song now?" Grandpa asked.

Tommie looked around. All the others were over in a corner of the yard talking. Tommie was too shy to sing for a group of strangers, even if they were all her aunts and uncles, but she didn't mind singing for her grandparents and Delores. She sang a little song she had learned in school.

> "Pretty maid, come along,
> You shall hear the fond song,
> The sweet notes that the nightingale sings,
> You shall hear the fond tale,
> Of the sweet nightingale,
> As he sings in the valley below,
> As he sings in the valley below."

When she had finished singing both verses of the song Grandpa thanked her, and she and Delores went off on a tour of inspection.

Gay flowers filled every corner of Grandma's yard. After seeing them Tommie understood why Daddy loved flowers so much. As she and Delores stood admiring the hollyhocks, Aunt

Nola joined them. "Do you know how to make hollyhock dolls?" she asked.

Neither of the girls did, so Aunt Nola took one of the silky blossoms, stuck an unopened bud on the stem for a head, and then trimmed another flower to the right size and shape for a hat. Both Tommie and Delores were delighted with the doll.

"What I really came out for," said Aunt Nola, "was to find out if you girls wanted to go with me to get the ice cream. The boys are all off playing somewhere, so you girls may come with me if you'd like."

At the creamery the man in charge brought out a five-gallon can of ice cream that had been ordered the week before. Then he brought Tommie and Delores each an ice-cream cone.

When they got back with the ice cream, they saw that a long table had been set up in the yard. It was loaded with food. Tommie had never seen so much food in one place before, not even at a school picnic. Before anyone ate, however, one of the uncles had them all bow their heads while he said a prayer. Tommie was puzzled over this. Nobody she knew prayed before meals.

Maybe it was just because this was a special occasion. She soon forgot to wonder about it. Someone handed her a plate of food, and she went to sit under a tree with Delores to eat. The food tasted delicious to Tommie, and she ate so much that she felt sure she'd not want food again for at least a week.

After dinner Aunt Josie took the children out by the well and seating them in a circle, told them stories. Tommie always loved stories. Then Aunt Josie had them sing. Delores and Val knew all the songs, but Tommie didn't.

Later she asked Delores where she had learned the songs.

"We learned them in Sabbath School," said Delores. "Don't you go to Sabbath School?"

"No," said Tommie. "I have a friend named Lucinda and she goes to Sunday School. Is it something like that?"

"Yes, it's like Sunday School, only we go on Saturday," said Delores.

"What do you do there?" Tommie asked.

"We sing songs, and someone tells us stories, and we say verses from the Bible, and we have a Bible lesson every week," Delores replied.

"It sounds nice," Tommie said wistfully. She wished she could go. It would be fun to learn new songs and hear stories.

"It is nice," said Delores. "We try never to miss Sabbath School."

Val came up then to say the boys wanted them to join in a game of tag, so Tommie didn't learn any more about Sabbath School.

After they tired of playing tag, Tommie and Delores went into Grandma's bedroom and played with Uncle Al's baby girl. Her name was Dana, and she seemed to enjoy having Delores and Tommie there to play with her.

The afternoon passed, and Tommie's aunts and Grandma again loaded the table with food. Tommie had been sure after dinner that she couldn't eat another bite that day, but the running and playing had revived her appetite. She ate her fill, and then Daddy said it was time to go home and do the chores.

Aunt Nola came and put a hand on Tommie's shoulder. "Your grandpa wants to know if you'll come and sing that little song for him again before you go home. Will you, Tommie?"

This time most of the aunts and uncles gathered around as Tommie sang the song about the nightingale, but she wasn't so shy now. She'd had all day to get acquainted with them, so she didn't mind singing while they stood around.

Then the good-byes were said, and Tommie and her family got into Uncle Don's car to be taken home. All during the ride home Tommie thought over the happy time she'd had that day. How nice it would be, she said to herself, if Delores lived close enough for them to play together all the time. Then she could learn more about Sabbath School.

While they did the chores that evening, Tommie's stomach began to feel uneasy. Mamma looked at her and said, "Are you sick, Tommie? Your face is so pale, every freckle stands out as plain as can be!"

"My stomach aches a little," Tommie said.

"Did you eat too much today?" asked Daddy.

Mamma answered for her. "I don't think she did," she said. "It must be all the excitement, and the food was richer than she's accustomed to."

"I'll give you some medicine for your stomach," said Daddy. "Then you can go to bed." He filled a teaspoon with sugar and dropped two or three drops of camphor onto it. "Here, now, Tommie, eat this. It will help that stomachache!"

Tommie took the remedy gratefully. It tasted good. She got into bed, and after a while her stomach felt better. Trying to remember the words of one of the songs Aunt Josie had taught them that day, she drifted off to sleep.

Winter in the Ozarks

Fall arrived at last with brisk days and cool nights. Maple trees in the pasture flamed with bright red and gold leaves. Then the leaves turned brown and dropped to the fields.

The morning after the first frost, Tommie and Bud ran to the persimmon trees on the hill. Now the bitter, puckery fruit would be good to eat. Tommie and Bud loved persimmons. Some trees had soft, pulpy persimmons, and some had hard, firm persimmons that were almost all sugar. The persimmons would be good all winter.

Snow fell the Saturday after Thanksgiving. For two days it snowed, big feathery flakes that turned the hills into a fairyland. At night the wind howled, sifting the snow on the hills into huge piles. But the house and farm buildings nestled in the protected hollows, and the wind hardly bothered the snow there.

Early Monday morning Daddy climbed up onto the ridge. When he came back, he stamped the snow off his boots, put another stick of wood into the heating stove, and said, "The roads are drifted pretty bad up on top. The school bus won't be able to get through, or likely the mail carrier, either."

Tommie felt disappointed. She hadn't missed a day of school all year and hoped to get another Perfect Attendance Certificate. Well, it couldn't be helped. Their little farm community had no snowplow or tractor to remove the snow, so until at least part of it melted there would be no traffic on the road. Even if the mail carrier did get through, a loaded school bus could not make it to the top of the steep hills.

As days passed, Bud and Tommie grew tired of staying inside. Tommie had read every book and magizine at least twice, and Bud was tired of games. When they went outside, the freezing air soon sent them shivering back inside.

"What can we do, Mamma?" Tommie asked one day in desperation.

"Come into the kitchen. I've just had an idea," said Mamma. In the kitchen she got out sugar and flavoring and eggs.

"Beat the eggs, will you, Tommie, while I measure out some milk?" she said. When Tommie's beater made stiff little peaks in the egg whites, Mamma mixed them with the other ingredients. She poured the mixture into a gallon bucket. With the lid fastened in place, Mamma handed the bucket to Bud.

"Now," she said, "go bury that in the snowdrift on the north side of the house. That will be ice cream for supper."

Somehow the idea of making their own ice cream brightened things considerably. Daddy came in shortly afterward and brightened things even more. He had spent the entire morning at the barn. Now be carried a sled he had made. "There are two more sleds outside," he said. "Who wants to try them out?"

"Me! Me! Me!" shouted Tommie, Bud, and Becky Jane. Since there was no traffic on the road, they could sled safely there. Their sleds sometimes ran off the road into the buckbrush thickets, tumbling the riders off into the deep snow, but even that was fun!

All afternoon the sleds zipped along the road. Now and then the children had to take time out to come in and get warm and dry by the heating stove, but the fun of sledding soon brought them outside again.

At last it was chore time and then suppertime. Mamma had made a cake, and Bud and Tommie dug the ice cream out of the snowdrift. Tommie could not remember anything ever tasting so good as that ice cream.

For nine days nothing but the car of the mail carrier traveled the road. Then one day he left word at each house. "The school bus is going to try to get through tomorrow."

Tommie jumped up and down with excitement when the yellow school bus stopped in front of the door next morning. She loved school and hated to miss even one day.

At the foot of the big hill near Tommie's house Mr. Willis stopped the bus. Turning to the children he said, "This hill is pretty slippery. It will be safer if you get out and walk. Wait up at the top."

Everyone left the bus and walked up the hill. When they had all reached the top Mr. Willis started up. Three times he tried but stopped before reaching the top. On the fourth try he succeeded. By this time Tommie's hands and feet felt frozen.

Late for school, but happy to be back, the children piled into their classrooms. Tommie found that she had not missed much schoolwork because school had closed for four days. The other buses hadn't been able to make their rounds either. Neither had the children been counted absent, since it was not their fault the buses couldn't get through. Tommie still had a chance to get her Perfect Attendance Certificate.

Christmas drew near. The last day before Christmas vacation the schoolrooms had their parties. They had drawn names, and all the brightly wrapped packages had been accumulating under the trees in the schoolrooms. As the gifts were passed out, Tommie unwrapped a small package with her name on it. Watercolors! What fun they would be during the long winter evenings. The tag said "From Reatha." Then she watched as Bud's friend, Paul, opened the green woolen mittens Tommie had brought as her gift. Paul grinned as he tried the mittens on. "Thanks, Tommie," he called. "My old ones had holes in them." Tommie felt pleased that he liked them. Then she looked at her new watercolors. She decided that giving presents was as much fun as receiving them.

Several days after Christmas vacation started, Mamma said to Tommie, "Lucinda's parents have invited us down to visit them this evening after supper. I wish you'd iron a dress for Becky Jane and braid her hair."

Tommie put the irons on the kitchen stove to get hot. She sprinkled Becky Jane's pink gingham dress and rolled it in a towel. Then she took a hot iron and, after running it carefully over an old cloth so that no stove black would rub off on the dress, she began to iron. When the first iron cooled she put it back on the stove and got another one. When she had finished, she carefully hung the little dress away.

That evening the family walked together down the road to Lucinda's house. Snow still covered the ground, but the air felt warm for a winter evening. Daddy's lantern made a bright pool of light on the road as they walked along.

"Come into my bedoom, Tommie, said Lucinda when Tommie arrived. "Guess what! We're going back home to spend Christmas with my grandparents! Oh, I just love Christmas in the city!"

"Tell me what it's like," said Tommie.

"The stores are all decorated with lights for weeks ahead of time," began Lucinda. "The Christmas lights are strung up in the streets, and when they turn them on at night it looks beautiful. I just can't describe it. People ice-skate on a pond in the park, and everybody has parties. It's loads of fun!"

Tommie tried to imagine what the decorations and lights looked like.

"You find so many things to buy in the stores, you can hardly make up your mind," Lucinda went on. "People crowd the streets, and loudspeakers in front of the stores play Christmas carols all day long."

That night as they walked home, Tommie thought of what Lucinda had told her. The moon shown so bright Daddy didn't even light the lantern now. Tommie thought, "Who needs streetlights? The moonlight on the snow is probably just as pretty. And a catalog is as much fun as going shopping in a store!" Off in the woods an owl began to hoot. Tommie grinned. "That owl isn't much of a substitute for loudspeakers playing Christmas carols, but I think Christmas in the country is just as good as Christmas anywhere else!"

Christmas came and went, but the snow and cold weather persisted. The older people kept saying they hadn't seen a winter like it in years. Daddy came in from the woodpile one evening and said, "Our supply of wood is going much faster than usual. At this rate we won't have enough to last the rest of the winter. Tommie and Bud still have a week of vacation left. I think I'll start cutting more wood while they are home to help."

The next morning Tommie and Bud went with Daddy to the woods across the road from the barn. Daddy cut down a small tree and chopped the branches off. Then he showed Tommie and Bud how to place it in the "V-shaped braces he'd made. He told them to saw the log into small lengths for the heating stove.

Tommie took one end of the saw and Bud took the other. Back and forth, back and forth they sawed. They piled the lengths in a stack for Daddy to haul to the house later. Daddy built a fire and told them they could stop and get warm whenever they felt cold and tired. Then he went off and cut down more trees and dragged them to where Tommie and Bud worked. How grateful they were for their new gloves.

After four days of wood sawing Daddy decided they had enough wood cut to last the rest of the winter.

Neighboring families found their woodpiles dwindling too, and the men trudged through the snow to cut trees from the woods. Often they stopped at Tommie's house to get warm as they left the woods. They knew Daddy would welcome their visits, and Mamma always gave them a bowl of hot homemade vegetable soup and a slice of her raised bread.

The soup kettle simmered continually at the back of the kitchen stove, and every day Mamma added something more to it. It was wonderful soup—nothing tasted better than a steaming hot bowlful of it when Tommie came in half frozen from helping with the chores.

Late one afternoon Mr. Hermann stopped by to get warm. He finished the soup and sat back. "That was mighty good!" he said to Mamma. "It would have been wonderful to have during the winter my partner and I lived in Alaska."

"Tell us about it," Tommie begged.

"Well, it got really cold up there, I can tell you," he began. "We cut logs in weather so cold we were in constant danger of having our hands and feet frozen—our noses too! I know it was at least forty degrees below zero a great deal of the time. We lived on bread and beans almost all winter. We had used most of our supplies by spring, so we decided to go to the trading post and sell some maple sugar we'd made.

"I went up into the attic of our cabin to get the sugar. My partner stood below to take the sack when I had it filled. Those cakes of sugar weighed about five pounds each, and one of them slipped out of my hand. I yelled 'Look out!' but instead of getting out of the way my pal looked up to see what I was yelling about! That cake of maple sugar hit him right on the ear and nearly tore it off his head!"

"What did you do?" asked Bud.

"I came down and bandaged up his ear as best I could and then we took our sugar and went on to the trading post."

"Was there a doctor at the trading post to sew the ear back on?" Bud questioned.

"No," said Mr. Hermann. "Besides, it took us two days to get to the trading post, and it would have been too late then to sew it on."

"Did the ear grow back on by itself?" Tommie asked.

"Yes, it did," Mr. Hermann answered. "It grew on a bit crooked—every time it rained that ear got filled up with rainwater!" He smiled, and Tommie couldn't tell whether he was teasing or not. It was a good story, anyhow. All Mr. Hermann's stories were good.

Finally the snow melted, and the days began to lengthen. One afternoon early in March as Tommie went after the cows, a tiny spot of blue caught her eyes. A single bluet bloomed in the brown grass by the barnyard gate. Tommie pulled up the little plant, roots and all, and cupped it in her hands. She held it up to her nose and took a deep breath. One little bluet doesn't have much fragrance, but it contained all the promise of spring. Winter had passed!

Only One Loyal Friend

War raged between the United States and the Axis powers, and the boys at Tommie's school debated endlessly about whether the Army, the Navy, the Marines, or the Air Corps was better. They tried to decide which they wanted to join, a decision they had about six years to make since it would be that long before they reached draft age. Some of the impatient boys wished the time to hurry by so they could join before the war ended; others hoped they'd be allowed to finish high school before their draft call came.

The girls didn't want to be left out either. Some talked about quitting school when they were sixteen to get jobs in the big-city defense plants. They could earn a lot of money, they said, and then come back and finish high school when the war was over. When Tommie told Mamma what the girls were saying, she said, "Tommie, the girls who quit high school now will likely never come back to finish. An education is too important to neglect just to make a lot of money for a short time."

Even some members of Tommie's family were lured away by the money offered by war work. Aunt Bonnie and Uncle John rented out their land to a tenant farmer and moved to California to work. The family discussed it solemnly as letters came back from them telling of their new life in a big city.

"They live in an apartment in a building with lots of other families. I don't see how they can stand it," said Granny.

Tommie looked out the window at the hills and trees and wondered how it would feel to see nothing there but buildings and people. She felt sure she wouldn't like it.

Ellamae and her two brothers came inside the warm house to wait for the school bus. Their speech was quaint, and their clothes looked old.

Uncle Bill echoed her thoughts. "There'd be too many people there to suit me," he said. "I'm afraid they'd cramp my style. Nope, I guess I'll stay here and farm!"

"And can you imagine having to buy every bite you eat?" asked Mamma. "I've never had to buy a vegetable—not even so much as a single carrot—in all the years I've been married, except maybe a few potatoes toward the end of winter."

"I just don't believe it's worth it," Grandpa said, "to leave your family and kin, and go off and work for money that will only have to be paid out for groceries anyhow!" Everyone agreed with him.

Posters sprang up on the bulletin boards at school—posters that said "A Slip of the Lip May Sink a Ship!" and "Don't Start Rumors!" Tommie wondered what she could say that would sink a ship, or what kind of rumor she wasn't supposed to start.

One day a train crew saw a low-flying airplane disappear behind a hill. They were certain it had crashed and notified the nearest air base. Planes searched the area for two days but found no plane. Further checking revealed that no base had a plane missing. Tommie's class discussed this event in citizenship period one day as an example of the trouble an unfounded rumor could cause. After that Tommie understood better what it meant to start rumors.

One day at school Lucinda whispered excitedly, "See, we have a new girl in class this morning. Over there—sitting behind Viola."

At noon Tommie noticed that the new girl wore her dresses a longer length than the rest of them did, and her hair, instead of being curled, was drawn back into a bun at the nape of her neck. Her name was Ellamae Hankins, and she appeared very shy.

That afternoon Ellamae and her two younger brothers boarded the same bus Tommie did after school. The three newcomers sat together without saying a word to anyone, but Tommie noticed that they got off the bus at the corner where the ridge road joined the main road less than a quarter of a mile from her own home.

Tommie mentioned them to Mamma when she got home. "I've heard that a family has moved into that little house about two miles down the ridge road," Mamma replied. "We'll have to go see them soon and see if there's anything we can do for them."

The next morning Ellamae and her two little brothers waited at the comer for the school bus. "Come sit by me, Ellamae," Tommie called as the trio climbed on the bus.

"Thank ye kindly," Ellamae said with a shy smile. "Here, Jakie and Robbie, you set hyar behind me so's I kin keep an eye on ye!"

"Do you live in that little house down the ridge road?" Tommie asked.

"Yes," replied Ellamae. "We'uns come up hyar so Pa could do carpenter work on that thar new air base bein' built in Compton. Seein's how we'uns always lived in the woods before, we'uns was plumb grateful to find that little house. Pa, he lives by the air base and only comes home weekends." She stopped, her face pink. That had been a long speech for a girl as shy as Ellamae.

"Do you like school?" Tommie asked.

"Oh, yes," smiled Ellamae. "I've always loved school!"

In the days to come Tommie discovered that Ellamae really did love school. Before long she stood near the top of the class in everything but English. No amount of coaxing by the English teacher could get Ellamae to change her way of speech. She always acted polite about it, but some native stubbornness kept her from changing her words one bit.

"I know there's a better way of speakin'," she confided to Tommie one day, "but we'uns has always talked this way, an' somehow I jest don't get so homesick for back home if'n I kin keep a-talkin' like I always have. Besides, if'n I change how I talk, when we'uns did go back home, people 'ud say that thar Hankins gal had shore got stuck-up the time she was away!"

One cold day Tommie suggested to Ellamae and her two brothers that, instead of waiting at the comer for the bus, they take a shortcut through the pasture and wait inside her warm house.

"It won't be a bit farther to walk if you cut across our pasture," she said, "and Mamma would be glad to have you!"

"Thank ye kindly," said Ellamae, "but we'uns cain't!"

"We'uns is scared," piped Robbie.

"Scared?" repeated Tommie. "Why, what are you afraid of?"

"Well, hain't you'uns the ones as has that black cat?" demanded Jakie.

"Yes," replied Tommie, knowing they were referring to Kitty, her coal-black pet.

"Well, if'n that cat was to cross our path, we'uns 'ud have all kinds of bad luck," the little boy explained.

Tommie changed her mind about smiling when she saw how serious the three were. Instead she said, "Is that right?"

"Yes'm, hit is!" declared Jakie. "Why, we'uns had an uncle oncet, and a black cat crossed his path, and he knowed he shoulda turned around and gone straight home, only he didn't 'cause he was in a hurry, and you know what?"

"No, what?" asked Tommie.

"Well, he had an accident and broke his laig, that's what!"

"If I keep Kitty shut up in a bedroom all the time you're there, will you come and wait at my house?" Tommie asked.

The two boys looked at Ellamae. She nodded. "I reckon we kin," she said, "if'n you'uns be sure not to let the cat git out!"

Later she said apologetically to Tommie, "I hain't sure as how these things is so, but—but it's how we'uns has been taught."

After that the Hankins children waited for the bus at Tommie's house, and she had opportunity to find out other things they had been taught.

One morning Jakie watched Tommie's mother as she dipped warm water from the reservoir of the stove. "Do you have a horseshoe in thar?" he asked, pointing to the reservoir.

" A horseshoe?" asked Mamma. "No, I don't."

"We'uns always keeps a horseshoe in the reservoir of our stove," he stated. "Hit's a shore way to keep the hawks from gittin' the chickens."

"I've never had trouble with hawks bothering my chickens," smiled Mamma.

"I expect you will, come summer," he prophesied darkly, "an' if'n you do, you just remember what I told ye!"

Tommie and Mamma had a long talk one day about the funny things the Hankins children believed.

"Don't you ever, ever make fun of them, Tommie, for believing those things," said Mamma. "Besides being rude and impolite, it would just make them more stubborn in their beliefs."

"But, Mamma, you and I both know that those things aren't so," protested Tommie.

"Yes, we do," agreed Mamma; "but we'll show them far more by example than we can by words. If they see that the hawks don't bother my chickens even though I don't keep a horseshoe in the reservoir of the stove, or if they see that you don't have bad luck, even though Kitty crosses your path a dozen times a day, they will begin to wonder about it all."

"Ellamae seems to be wondering about it already," said Tommie.

"Ellamae's a smart little girl. She will grow more and more away from these things as she gets older, I think," replied Mamma. "You, Tommie, are more fortunate than you realize. Your grandparents were both schoolteachers, and your Daddy has had two years of college. That has been a big help to you. In return, more will be expected of you than will be expected of those children who are brought up in homes ruled by superstition." Mamma paused a moment, then changed the subject. "By the way, Tommie, I want to send to town for some sewing-machine needles tomorrow. Can you get them for me?"

"Yes, Mamma! I'm sure I can get permission to go to town at noon."

Tommie's teacher gave her permission to go to town the next day during noon recess. Her errand finished, she was hurrying back to school when she heard an airplane. She glanced up at the sky, trying to locate it. "It's probably in the clouds," she thought. Suddenly the sound of the motor changed—Tommie looked to the northeast in time to see a dark shape hurtling toward the ground.

There was a dull, far-away crash and a column of black smoke rose to the sky. It was at least a mile away, Tommie thought.

She stood rooted to the ground, her knees weak. "Oh, I hope the pilot is all right!"

Then she thought, "I'll have to tell someone. No one else may have noticed." Panting, breathless, she reached the schoolroom door, then paused to try to calm herself before entering. She would tell Miss Winters, her teacher for that period, and let her decide who to notify.

The other students had just taken their seats when Tommie entered.

"Miss Winters, Miss Winters," gasped Tommie, still out of breath, "I saw a plane fall!"

"Please take your seat, Tommie," directed the teacher calmly.

"But, Miss Winters, shouldn't we do something—notify someone?"

"Your imagination is working overtime, Tommie," said Miss Winters. "Now, go to your seat!"

"But, Miss Winters, I saw it!" Tommie insisted. "I heard it first and it didn't sound right, and I saw it falling!"

"Tommie," said Miss Winters kindly, "I realize you think you saw a plane fall, but those things just don't happen here!"

"What kind of a plane was it, Tommie?" demanded one of the boys.

"I don't know—I don't know one kind of plane from another. But I do know I saw one fall!" Tommie answered.

"Let's speak no more of it," said Miss Winters. "We've all seen the posters that say 'Don't Start Rumors,' and this is exactly the kind of thing those posters try to prevent!"

Tommie couldn't study. She kept wondering about the pilot of the plane—had he had time to bail out? Was he out in the woods somewhere, injured, hoping for help that would never come unless she could convince someone his plane had really crashed?

At recess she turned to say something to Viola. To her surprise Viola said coldly, "Don't speak to me! I have no use for troublemakers!"

Tommie walked over to Reatha and Margaret, but the two girls turned their backs as if Tommie didn't exist.

Tommie thought of Lucinda. They had been best friends for several years. Lucinda would not treat her as the others had. Lucinda was at her desk reading, but at Tommie's approach, she stood up deliberately, and put her book away.

"Lu—Lucinda," began Tommie imploringly.

"Excuse me, Tommie, I'm busy!" And Lucinda walked away.

Tommie was crushed. She stood looking out the window, gazing into the distance. A voice spoke at her side. "I heerd them other girls a-talkin'," said Ellamae as she took Tommie's hand. "If'n you saw that thar plane go down, don't you let them bother you none. Hit'll all come out all right!"

Tommie smiled at her gratefully. "You're a real, true friend, Ellamae," she said unsteadily.

During the last period of the day, Tommie, still smarting from the treatment she'd received from her classmates, sat sullenly.

"I'll show them," she thought. "Instead of coming to school tomorrow I'll get off the schoolbus in town and I'll go to hunt that plane! I'll hunt until I find it, and I'll never come back to this school again until I do find it!"

As Tommie walked in from school, Mamma looked up from her chair where she sat mending. "There has been real excitement in the neighborhood this afternoon, Tommie," she said. "An airplane crashed over in the woods and your daddy's just got back from where it hit!"

Tommie buried her head in Mamma's lap and burst into tears. Mamma looked startled. Finally Tommie controlled herself enough to pour out the whole story to Mamma—how she'd seen the plane crash but hadn't been able to get anyone to do anything about it; how the girls, even Lucinda, wouldn't speak to her because of it, and only Ellamae had remained her friend; and how she had determined to go find the plane herself the next day.

"Why, Tommie, you've been a really brave girl today," exclaimed Mamma. "Not many people would have been so sure of themselves in the face of the treatment you received. And not many would have had the courage to go alone to hunt for a plane nobody else believed had crashed! As it happened, lots of people saw that plane fall. Your daddy saw it from where he was working in the field, and when he finally got to where it had crashed, there were already about twenty men there!"

"The pilot, Mamma?" questioned Tommie. "Was he all right?"

"Yes," Mamma reassured her. "He came down into the trees and was only scratched a bit. He's already back at the air base."

The next day in school Miss Winters rapped the desk for silence and said, "I want to apologize to Tommie for what happened yesterday. I refused to listen to her when she had something important to say. I was wrong, and I am sorry!" She smiled at Tommie, and then continued, "If any of the rest of you have anything to say to Tommie about this matter you may tell her at recess."

When recess came, the girls tried to tell Tommie how sorry they were for their conduct the day before. She smiled and said it was all right, and from their expressions of relief she knew they hadn't been sure she'd accept their apologies. She took a deep breath. It was good to be all friends again, but she felt she'd never have another friend as loyal as Ellamae.

"Mamma, she may talk and dress funny, and believe in all sorts of superstitious things, but I'll always love Ellamae for what she did yesterday," Tommie declared that evening.

"Yes, I imagine you will," agreed Mamma. "The friend who believes in us when everyone else turns away is the one we remember longest and cherish the most. I hope you'll always try to be that kind of friend."

"I'll try, Mamma," said Tommie. "Ellamae has already set me a good example!"

School Buses Won't Wait

Tommie dashed in from the school bus one day in early April. "We're home, Mamma," she announced as usual. Bud and Becky Jane came trooping in behind her.

Mamma came in from the kitchen. "Put on your work clothes," she said, "and then I'll tell you what to do."

Tommie changed into overalls and red plaid shirt, and Bud put on older clothes.

"Bud, you are to go over and pile brush where Daddy is clearing new ground. Tommie, Daddy wants you to go pick some mushrooms for supper. He says he saw some over in that hollow the other side of Whippoorwill Ridge."

Mamma did not have to ask if Tommie knew which of the wild mushrooms were good to eat and which ones were not. She knew Daddy had carefully trained Tommie in this matter.

"May I go with Sissy?" Becky Jane asked.

Mamma looked inquiringly at Tommie. "I like company," said Tommie. "She may come along."

"All right, Becky Jane. You may go along with Sissy," said Mamma.

The two girls walked hand in hand down toward the barn, ducked under the fence, and entered the woods. The first hill they climbed had no name, but the second had been called Whippoor-will Ridge ever since the summer Tommie and Bud had found whippoorwill eggs at the top of the hill. All summer they had watched the eggs and the two baby birds, being very careful never to touch either.

In the hollow on the other side of the ridge Tommie began looking for the mushrooms. They were hard to see, for they blended in with the dried leaves on the ground. They were morels, commonly known in Tommie's area as "molli-moochers," and they looked like little grayish-brown pine trees. They tasted delicious fried.

Here one and there one—back and forth Tommie went picking them. She looked carefully around the bases of the trees and beside the rocks.

Now and then Becky Jane would come and say, "Is this a good mushroom, Sissy?" and Tommie would either say, "Yes, that's a fine one—put it in the bucket," or "No, that one's not good. Throw it away." Tommie had the bucket nearly full when she realized that Becky Jane hadn't brought a mushroom to her for some time. She looked up. The little girl was not in sight.

"Becky! Becky Jane!" Tommie called, but there was no answer.

"Becky! Becky Jane, where are you?" Tommie called louder.

Becky Jane's voice came from down the hollow. "I'm coming! I found some mushrooms." She came trudging up the hollow, holding up her skirt. "See, I got a whole lot!"

Tommie went to meet her. Sure enough, Becky Jane had found a big bunch of the morels, and, having nothing to put them into, she had carried them in her skirt. Tommie took off her straw hat, and Becky dumped the mushrooms into it.

"Becky Jane, you'll be an expert mushroom hunter yet, you just wait and see," said Tommie, giving her little sister a hug. "Now let's get the cows and take them home as we go!"

Tommie carried the bucket, and Becky Jane carried the bat, and together they found the cows. As they drove the cows home Tommie heard a noise in the dry leaves nearby. She put a hand on Becky Jane's shoulder and stopped her. Becky looked up questioningly.

"I hear a noise in the leaves," Tommie whispered. "Let's be quiet and see what it is."

"A snake?" breathed Becky Jane.

"No, I don't think so. Sh-h-h, now!"

The noise came again. It was too loud and deliberate to be either a snake or a lizzard. Tommie looked around. Another rustle in the leaves, and then she spotted the cause.

"There it is, Becky Jane—look!" and she pointed to the pile of leaves a few feet away.

"Oh, a terrapin!" exclaimed Becky Jane. An old box tortoise, or terrapin, as Tommie and Becky called him, watched them solemnly. Becky Jane ran to pick him up. He drew legs, head, and tail into his shell, and shut himself inside with a hiss. Becky Jane turned him over and looked at the underside of his shell.

"Sissy, something is carved on this terrapin's shell," she said.

Tommie took the terrapin and looked where Becky Jane pointed. There, carved on the bottom of the shell, were the letters "T. G." and a date showing that the carving had been done eight years before.

"Those are my initials," Tommie said wonderingly, "but I certainly never carved them there. Why, eight years ago I was just your age, Becky Jane, and I wasn't allowed to carve on anything, any more than you are now!"

"Let's take him home and show Mamma," suggested Becky Jane, so the girls gathered up their mushrooms and Tommie also carried the terrapin.

"Look at this, Mamma," said Tommie, showing the initials on the terrapin's shell. "Those are my initials, aren't they? Only, I didn't put them there. Do you suppose someone else has the same initials?"

"We can ask Daddy when he comes in," Mamma suggested. "Maybe he'll know."

"Daddy, do you know anything about this terrapin with my initials on him?" Tommie asked when Daddy came in from the field.

Daddy took the terrapin and looked. "Well, well, well!" he exclaimed with a smile. "Yes, I believe I do know something about this old fellow. About eight years ago, when you were Becky Jane's age, you went with me one evening to hunt the cows. We caught this terrapin and you asked me to carve your name on his shell. That was too much carving, but I did put your initials and the date on there, and here he is, eight years later."

"Daddy, will you carve my initials on a terrapin someday?" Becky Jane asked.

"Why, of course, Becky," said Daddy. "Do you want me to put yours on here with Tommie's, or do you want a terrapin of your own?"

"Put mine on with Sissy's," answered Becky Jane. "I might not find another terrapin for a long time."

"You'll find terrapins all over the farm this summer," smiled Daddy, "but if you want your initials on this one, I'll put them on there now." Taking out his pocket knife, he carved "B. J. G." and the date right beside Tommie's initials. "Now then, girls," he said, "you can take him up the hill and turn him loose."

"Oh, Daddy, could I take him to school tomorrow and then turn him loose tomorrow afternoon when I go for the cows?" asked Tommie.

"Yes, that will be all right," Daddy said, so Tommie put the terrapin in a box and went about her work.

The next morning when she got on the school bus Mr. Willis eyed the box curiously. "Big lunch you've got there, Tommie," he said.

"This isn't my lunch, Mr. Willis," Tommie giggled. "This is a terrapin. Daddy carved my initials on his shell eight years ago—see?—and I found him last night when I went after the cows."

The terrapin with Tommie's initials on it caused a big sensation at school. The teacher told the class that terrapins live for many years and don't usually stray far from their own feeding territory. She said that maybe someday when Tommie grew up her children would find that terrapin with their mother's initials on it.

By noon the terrapin had become so used to the schoolroom that he didn't bother to shut himself inside his shell every time one of the pupils came near. Ellamae's little brother Jakie stood and watched cautiously as the children put bread and fruit in the box for the terrapin to eat.

"You'uns had better watch out," he warned, "'cause if'n that thaing was to bite you he wouldn't turn loose until hit thundered, not even if'n you cut his head off'n him!"

When school let out that afternoon Lucinda and Tommie sat on the back steps of the schoolhouse. Mr. Willis had to take two busloads of children home, and Tommie and Lucinda were in the second group. Usually Ellamae joined them, but today she was home helping her mother with the new baby.

"Did I tell you we are going to move?" Lucinda asked casually.

Tommie's heart sank. She had thought Mr. Morris had been doing much better on the farm, and they had all seemed so happy and settled.

"Oh, no!" she protested. "Oh, I'll just miss you so much! It isn't right for you to go away and leave me now that we've been good friends for so long!"

Lucinda laughed. "Oh, I'm not going far! Daddy bought Mr. Webb's farm, and we're going to move there. See, we'll be only two miles away."

"Lucinda!" Tommie scolded. "How could you be so mean and scare me so? Why didn't you say right away you were going to move to Mr. Webb's farm?"

"I would have," said Lucinda innocently, "only you started fussing so much I didn't get a chance!"

"Well, I'm glad you're going to be only two miles away, even though it is farther than you live from me now," said Tommie. "Anyhow, I didn't know Mr. Webb's farm was for sale. Where is he moving to?"

"He's going to quit farming, said Lucinda, "and move to Texas to live with his daughter."

"It's a nice farm—one of the nicest in the community," commented Tommie thoughtfully.

"Yes, it is," agreed Lucinda. "Mamma says—oh, Tommie, look!" She grabbed Tommie's arm and pointed down the road toward town. As Tommie looked the yellow school bus pulled onto the road and disappeared with the second load of students. They had been left behind!

"Oh, my!" said Tommie. She had never been careless enough before to let the bus leave her, but other children had. She and Lucinda stared at each other.

"The least he could have done was wait for us," Lucinda finally said.

"Yes, but think of all the other children he has to take home," replied Tommie. "Well, there's nothing to do but walk!" she added. "Five whole miles," she thought to herself. "Mamma and Daddy aren't going to like this one bit."

"That's a long way," Lucinda echoed her thoughts, "and I have to take my books so I can do my homework!"

"So do I," said Tommie, "but that isn't all. I'm going to cut through the fields until I get to the other side of town. I'm not going to let the kids who live in town have a chance to laugh at me just because I missed the bus. You know how they are!"

"I wouldn't care about that," protested Lucinda. "It's so much easier to walk on the road than it is through the fields."

"Well, I care about it," replied Tommie, "and I'm going through the fields." Lucinda reluctantly followed Tommie across a field.

Reaching the other side of town, the girls climbed through a fence back onto the road. The walk would have been fun if they hadn't felt so guilty about missing the bus. They both knew their parents wouldn't worry, for the roads were safe to travel, but Tommie knew it would make more work for the other members of the family if she wasn't there to do her share.

A warm April sun beat down as they hurried along the road. After a while Lucinda said, "Let's rest awhile," so they sat down under a tree. Lucinda was not as used to walking long distances as Tommie. "These books are certainly heavy," she sighed.

"I know," said Tommie. "Mine are too. Besides that, I'm carrying this terrapin."

"Why don't you turn him loose right here?" suggested Lucinda. "Then you wouldn't have to carry him any farther."

"No, sir!" replied Tommie vigorously. "This terrapin has lived on our farm for no telling how many years, and I'm not going to turn him loose in a strange place now!"

"Well, you could turn him loose and see how long it takes him to find his way home , Lucinda said.

Tommie considered for a minute. "No," she decided, " maybe terrapins aren't like dogs. I read of a dog who found his way home after he'd been taken hundreds of miles away, but I don't think a terrapin could do it." She giggled. "Anyway, didn't you hear the teacher say that maybe someday my children would find this terrapin with my initials on it? Well, as slow as a terrapin walks, this one wouldn't get to our farm in time for my children ever to find him—maybe not even my grandchildren! And if we keep resting under this tree, we won't get there either!"

When they got to the Webb farm Lucinda looked at it longingly. "I wish we lived here now," she said. "Then I'd be home. As it is, I have another two and a half miles to walk!"

"And if you lived here I'd have to walk the next two miles alone," Tommie reminded her.

The sun seemed hotter and the road longer than Tommie remembered. She wished she were home so she could rest and get a drink. On the other hand she wished she wouldn't get home for hours, because she wanted to delay the scolding she knew she deserved. Now and then Tommie glanced at the sun, estimating the time and guessing what the family was doing at home.

As they passed the ridge road corner she guessed Daddy and Bud would be finishing the milking. She wasn't far wrong, for when she walked into the yard she saw them leaving the barn. She said good-bye to Lucinda and went into the house. Taking a dipper of water she drank and drank, then washed her hot, dusty face and turned to meet Mamma.

"Come into the front room, Tommie," said Mamma. "I want to talk to you."

" Yes, Mamma," answered Tommie.

They went into the living room and sat down. Mamma was silent for a few moments, as if wondering how to begin. Then she spoke.

"Tommie," she said, "you know that each member of this family has his share of responsibility, and today you failed to live up to yours. One thing we expect of you is that you come home on the school bus. When you didn't do that today, you put an added burden on the others in the family."

"Yes, I know," said Tommie. She didn't feel like looking at Mamma.

"Knowing you as I do, I imagine you gave this some thought on the way home, didn't you?"

"Yes, Mamma!"

"You're too big to spank, Tommie, but you will have to be punished. Since we all had to help do your work today, during the rest of this week, each day you'll have to do one job belonging to someone else, in addition to your own work. Tomorrow you can fill the woodbox for Bud; the next day you can feed the chickens morning and evening for me. There will be other jobs later in the week. Do you think that is fair?"

"Yes, Mamma!" Tommie thought sadly of her playtime gone for the rest of the week. Yet she knew it wasn't fair for the others to have to do extra work because of her carelessness, and then get nothing in return.

"Mamma?" she asked in a small voice.

"Yes, Tommie."

"May I go and turn the terrapin loose in the pasture now?"

"Did you carry that terrapin all the way home from school?" Mamma asked in surprise. "Why, I thought you'd turn him loose as soon as you got tired of carrying him!"

"Oh, no!" said Tommie earnestly. "This is his home. I couldn't just turn him loose in a strange place."

Mamma smiled. "That shows you aren't completely irresponsible, Tommie," she said, "but it puzzles me how a girl with eyes sharp enough to spot mushrooms and find terrapins could miss something as big as a school bus!"

"It won't happen again, Mamma," said Tommie. "It's too long a walk home, and besides, I want to grow up to be responsible. I'll just try harder."

A Baby in the House

"Mamma, may I go over in the field and dig some sassafras roots for tea?" asked Tommie one Sunday morning. "I think it would be nice to have some for dinner."

"Yes, that's a good idea," replied Mamma. "Granny always says that sassafras tea is a good blood tonic in the spring."

"I don't know about it being a tonic, but I like to drink it," said Tommie.

"Maybe you'd have time to pick some greens for dinner," suggested Mamma. "It's early in the day yet!"

"Do you want to come along, Becky Jane?" asked Tommie.

"Yes, Sissy, I'm coming," Becky Jane answered.

Tommie took a large bucket and a small trowel, and she and Becky Jane went up the hill to the field. Sassafras sprouted all over the field, and Tommie dug until she had enough roots to make tea. She put them in the bottom of the bucket and covered them with a layer of sassafras leaves.

Then she and Becky Jane started picking wild greens. They found the young poke plants easiest, but they needed something to go with them. Tommie knew that lamb's-quarters grew by the barn lot, and she knew if she looked hard she could find other good plants too—clover, alfalfa, violet leaves, plantain, and even the tiny new leaves on the blackberry vines.

They spent almost all morning gathering enough greens for dinner. As Tommie picked them she showed Becky Jane which leaves were good to eat and which ones were not.

"I learned this by going with Mamma to pick greens when I was a little girl," she explained. "Someday you will have to pick the greens."

"Won't you always be here to help?" asked Becky Jane.

"Someday I may get to go away to college," Tommie answered.

"Oh!" Becky considered this for a moment, and then asked, "Will I have a little sister to teach too?"

"I don't know," replied Tommie.

"I hope I do," said Becky Jane.

When they had packed the bucket tight with greens, the girls went to the house. Tommie took the greens to the spring and washed them, examining each leaf for dirt or insects. She also scrubbed the sassafras roots she had dug for tea.

Lucinda came to play with Tommie after dinner, and Bobby Pender from the next farm came to see Bud. The four children decided to play "Give Me a Wave." They chose Tommie to be "it," and while she hid her eyes and counted to a hundred, they ran to hide. Whenever Tommie found a player she sent him to her base. If he could find one of the hidden players waving at him, he ran off to a new hiding place as soon as Tommie turned her back.

After Tommie, Bud became "it." He found all the players easily except Lucinda. The children looked in every direction but caught sight of no waving hand.

Suddenly Bobby began to giggle. "Look up on the roof," he whispered to Tommie. Through a hole in the roof where a shingle was missing, Tommie saw Lucinda's hand, waving wildly. As soon as Bud went around the corner of the house to hunt for Lucinda, Tommie and Bobby dashed off to hide.

Several times Bud captured Bobby and Tommie but a wave from the hand through the roof sent them off to hide again.

Not much light shone through the narrow attic windows where Lucinda hid, and she grew tired of waving through that hole in the roof. She had never been up there before and didn't know that the board floor didn't extend through the whole attic. The kitchen ceiling was only heavy cardboard. Carefully withdrawing her hand, she started to step away to find a more comfortable position for a while. Then one foot went right through the cardboard ceiling! She grabbed wildly and caught hold of an old trunk. Otherwise she would have plunged through to the kitchen floor below.

Mamma looked up startled as Lucinda's foot shot through the kitchen ceiling. She had been hearing the game outside, so she could guess what had happened. Lucinda came down the outside ladder she had used to get into the attic, and said shakily to the group at the peach tree, "I almost fell through the ceiling. My foot went through!"

"Don't worry about it," Tommie reassured her. "Daddy will fix it. He will have to go up to fix that hole in the roof, too."

"I'm tired of this game," Bud announced. "Come on, Bobby, let's go do something else."

The boys left Lucinda and Tommie sitting outside in the shade.

"Do you realize we have less than a month before the end of school?" Lucinda said. "I was sick the last week of school last year. Do we do anything special on the final day?"

"Sure we do. That's an important day," Tommie replied. "We have races and contests all morning on the ball field, and all the girls try to have new dresses to wear then."

"Do you have one?" asked Lucinda.

"Not this year," Tommie said. "Mamma says we can't afford it."

"If it's important, I'll just wear my Sunday dress," said Lucinda.

"I'll wear my good dress too," agreed Tommie.

When Tommie came home from school a few days later, Mamma said, "A package arrived for you today, Tommie."

"A package? For me?" asked Tommie in surprise.

"It's on the table," Mamma said.

The package was from Aunt Nola, and Tommie opened it eagerly. Inside were a yellow dress, a yellow slip to match, yellow anklets, a yellow hair ribbon, and a pair of shiny black patent slippers. Tommie stood speechless. Then she said, "They are beautiful! Just beautiful! All right in time for the last day of school!"

The last day of school arrived, and Tommie dressed carefully in her new yellow outfit. When Lucinda got on the bus, Tommie saw that she had a new dress too. The two girls looked at each other, then both spoke at once. "What a pretty new dress you have!" Then they both laughed.

"Aunt Nola sent mine to me," explained Tommie.

"My mother made mine and kept it as a surprise until this morning," said Lucinda.

Ellamae had a new dress, too. Lately her mother had been making her clothes more like the ones the other girls wore, and sometimes she even curled the girl's long blond hair. Tommie wished Ellamae would stop clinging to her old ways of speech too.

Coming home from school that afternoon the three girls sat together on the bus.

"Just think," said Lucinda. "The next time we ride this bus we'll be eighth-graders!"

"Yes," answered Tommie. "Next year we'll graduate."

"But we'uns'll see each other this summer, won't we?" asked Ellamae.

"Oh, yes," said Tommie. "It would be an awfully lonesome summer if I couldn't see both of you now and then."

When Tommie got off the bus, she found Granny visiting with Mamma. Granny and Grandpa had recently moved to Uncle Bill's house. He had brought Granny over that morning when he was on his way to town, and he would pick her up on his way home.

"We've been talking about you, Tommie," Granny said.

"What have I done now?" Tommie asked with a laugh. She knew Granny was teasing her.

"Your Aunt Bonnie and Uncle John are going on a vacation. They want us to go stay in their house and take care of their chickens, and they suggested that I take you along to keep me company. Do you want to go?"

"How long will they be gone?" Tommie asked.

"A week, they said," answered Granny.

"May I go, Mamma?" Tommie asked.

"Yes," replied Mamma. "I asked your daddy at noon, and he said you could!"

"Good!" declared Tommie. "When do we go?"

"Day after tomorrow," said Granny. "Bonnie will come for us that morning, and they will leave for their trip at noon. She'll pay you five dollars for your help too."

"I'd be glad to do it for nothing," said Tommie, "Just as a favor."

"Bonnie thinks your help is worth five dollars, and she wants you to have it," Granny said firmly.

"I could certainly use it," Tommie admitted.

At Aunt Bonnie's house all Tommie had to do was feed the chickens twice a day and keep Granny from getting lonesome. She didn't even have to go after the cows and help milk. A hired man did that.

Tommie's idea of keeping Granny company was to get her to sing all the ballads she knew and tell all the stories she could remember.

One day Granny told her about the first year she spent as a schoolteacher.

"I was just barely sixteen," Granny said. "Two of my boy students not only towered almost a foot above me, but were a year older than I besides. One day at noon they got into a fight. When school took up that afternoon, I called them to the front of the room and used a switch on them. They really didn't have to stand there and take their punishment, but they did. In fact, I believe they thought it was funny. That has been years and years ago, but whenever I see those men now, they always say, 'Good morning, teacher!'"

Home looked good to Tommie after having been away for a week. She had missed Mamma and Daddy, and Bud and Becky Jane too.

Two days later Uncle Bill came over with Granny again. "Tommie, you and Bud get your duds together—you're going to spend a week at my house," he called.

"But, Mamma, who will help you?" Tommie asked. She didn't want to go away again.

"I'm going to stay with your mother this week, Tommie," said Granny.

All that week Tommie helped out at Uncle Bill's farm. She helped Aunt Nellie with the housework and took care of her two little cousins. The work wasn't hard, but she wanted to be home.

At the end of the week Uncle Bill took them home. He left Granny at Tommie's house, though.

"Are you going to live with us now, Granny?" Bud asked.

"For a week or two, I guess," said Granny with a smile.

The next morning while the children played out in the yard, Daddy came and said, "Come on, youngsters, we're going over to Uncle Bill's house."

"But, Daddy, we were there all this past week!" said Tommie. "Can't we stay home now?"

"You'll only be there for the day," said Daddy in a tone of voice that meant Tommie was not to argue. "Come on, now, let's get started."

All the way over to Uncle Bill's house Tommie sulked. If it keeps on like this, she muttered to herself, I won't be home two weeks out of the whole summer!

As soon as they reached their destination, Daddy and Uncle Bill drove away in Uncle Bill's car. Tommie continued to sulk. She wanted to be home, and she didn't care who knew it. When gentle Aunt Nellie tried to talk to her, Tommie looked so cross that her aunt gave up and left her alone. Tommie even refused to eat dinner.

Daddy and Uncle Bill drove back into the yard in the early afternoon. "Come on, now, and get in the car," Daddy called. "We are going home."

When they got in the car, Uncle Bill said to Tommie, "Are you glad to be going home, Peanuts?"

Tommie refused to answer.

"Aren't you going to talk to me?" Uncle Bill asked.

Tommie shook her head stubbornly and snapped, "No!" She still felt mad. She knew she deserved a scolding for her attitude, and ordinarily Daddy would have given her one, but for some reason he just sat quietly as Uncle Bill drove on, and said nothing. Uncle Bill winked at Daddy and said, "If Peanuts knew about the new baby you have at home, I'll bet she'd talk."

"A new baby!" Tommie cried excitedly. "Oh, is there one—really? Is it a brother or sister?"

Neither Daddy nor Uncle Bill answered her.

"Well, come on—tell me!" she begged.

Uncle Bill turned to Daddy and grinned. "If Peanuts hadn't told me she wasn't going to talk to me, I'd swear I heard her asking me questions, as usual!"

"That is odd, isn't it?" Daddy laughed.

"Tell me," pleaded Tommie. "Is there really a baby at home, or are you just teasing me?"

"Are you talking to me, Peanuts?" asked Uncle Bill innocently.

"Yes, I am! Is the baby a boy or a girl?"

Uncle Bill relented a little. "I'll let your Daddy tell you," he said.

"The baby is a boy," said Daddy. "You'll see him in a minute—we're almost home."

The baby slept quietly in a basket by Mamma's bed. The children clustered about looking at him.

"He's so tiny," whispered Tommie. "What's his name?"

"We're going to call him Bill," answered Mamma.

"Am I going to get to stay home the rest of the summer and help take care of him?" Tommie inquired.

Daddy laughed. "If you're that anxious to stay home, I think we can arrange it," he said.

"It looks like it's going to be a pretty nice summer after all," Tommie said to herself, "even if it did start out bad."

In the lonely woods Tommie said her first prayer. She explained how much she wanted to make the trip, and how it depended on her uncle.

Prayer and a Surprise

The bell rang, signaling the end of the school day, and the eighth- and ninth-graders poured out into the corridor, talking excitedly.

The ninth-graders had planned an early fall field trip and had invited the eighth-graders to be their guests. Everyone was to be at school by seven-thirty the next morning, where a bus would be waiting. It would take them into the next state to visit a teachers' college, tour the school's museum and observatory, and then go through a bakery and a cannery. They would return to school at ten to be picked up by their parents.

No wonder the eighth-graders sounded excited. Few of them had ever been outside their own state, or seen an observatory, or been inside a museum! What treats to look forward to!

"Tommie, do you think you can go?" Lucinda asked. She knew Tommie could seldom attend school functions because her family lived back in the hills more than five miles from town, and a box wagon and team of mules was their only transportation.

Tommie looked doubtful. "If I had a way to get to the school and back I know I could go," she replied.

"Well," Lucinda said, "if your folks will let you walk the two miles to our house that early in the morning, you can ride in with us, but I'm going to spend the next night in town with Laura, so you'd have to find some other way home."

"Oh, thank you, Lu," beamed Tommie. "Maybe I can think of a way to get home. 'Bye now. Here comes my bus. See you tomorrow, I hope!"

Tommie's thoughts raced a mile a minute all the way home. Her uncle Bill had a car, and she knew he'd be glad to come to the school the next night to get her. After all, she was his favorite niece, a fact he made no effort to hide. He said he didn't approve of girls being called by boys' names, so he had always called her Peanuts instead of Tommie.

But how could she get a message to Uncle Bill, who lived three miles away?

"Maybe," she thought, "if I hurry and get my work done, and if I can find the cows without too much trouble, I will have time to walk over and see Uncle Bill myself."

Tommie outlined her plans to Mother. "And, Mamma," she finished, "don't you think I'll have time to go over to Uncle Bill's and see whether he will pick me up tomorrow night? I'll hurry."

"You'll have to ask your daddy, honey," Mamma replied.

"Why, I can't let you go over to Bill's tonight," Daddy said sternly. "Don't you remember what happened last night when you went after the cows?"

Tommie hung her head as her father continued, "The cows came in by themselves just before dark, and you didn't get home until nearly an hour later!"

Tommie remembered all too well. While hunting for the cows the previous evening she had found some tangled string and had promptly sat down on a log to untangle the snarls and wind the cord up neatly. She seldom could find a piece of string when she wanted one. All they ever had was what came on parcels.

So intent had she been on salvaging the tangled string that darkness fell almost before she knew it. Then she had jumped up and hurried through the woods, listening for cowbells, calling, searching, until she had finally given up and returned to the barnyard, only to find that the cows had gone home by themselves and the rest of the family had half the milking done. Her father scolded her severely for her misdeed, and she felt fortunate that the punishment had not been worse.

"But, Daddy, this is different," she ventured to say now.

"No, it isn't," he interrupted. "If you can't be trusted one day, how can I trust you the next? If I let you go to your uncle Bill's, perhaps you would come home when you say you would. On the other hand, you might get interested in something and not get home until midnight. No, I just can't take a chance on it. You can just consider this part of your punishment for neglecting your job yesterday. Now, go on and get the cows, and be quick about it!"

Tommie knew better than to argue with her father. She walked sadly to the pasture.

"Anyway," she mused aloud, "he didn't say I couldn't go tomorrow if I found a way to get home. Maybe Uncle Bill will come over to visit tonight, and I can tell him. And then—I wonder—maybe if I prayed, he might come. I've heard that God answers prayers. Lucinda and Dixie say it's true, and they both go to Sunday School. And that paper Aunt Nola used to send me-I think it was called *Little Friend*—had lots of stories about how God answers prayers, only they were all about little children. Maybe you are supposed to take care of yourself when you get to be as big as I am. Still, I think I'll try it."

She walked farther into the woods. "People kneel when they pray," she said to herself, "so that is what I'd better do."

She knelt down beside a small sassafras tree and said her first prayer. She explained that she didn't know much about praying, but she hoped God would understand. She told Him how badly she wanted to go on the trip the next day and how it all depended on Uncle Bill. She asked Him if He couldn't arrange somehow for her to see Uncle Bill that evening—she'd be so grateful if He would. She did know enough about prayer to end with Amen, after which she resumed her search for the cows. Before long she had them all in the barnyard.

Quickly finishing the rest of her work, she began to make preparations for the next day's trip. She pressed her good dress, put her hair up in curlers, polished her shoes, and counted her small hoard of spending money. All the while she kept listening for the sound of a car.

Her brother came in from finishing the outside chores. The family ate supper and washed the dishes, and still Uncle Bill hadn't come. Tommie grew more and more anxious.

Finally her father put down his newspaper and announced that it was time everyone went to bed. Shortly afterward he blew out the kerosene lamp, and the household settled down for the night. All except Tommie. She knew that any hope of seeing her uncle that night had gone. People didn't go visiting after bedtime—not in the country where work starts the next day before sunup.

Tommie felt disappointed—not just because she feared she'd miss the trip but because it seemed that God had not answered her prayer.

"Maybe there isn't much to this religion business, after all," she said to herself. Still, she thought wistfully, it would be nice to know that God answers prayers. Not just for the trip—she'd done without things like that before—but for something really important.

At last she fell asleep.

Suddenly she awakened. Someone pounded on the door, and a voice shouted, "Anybody home?"

That voice! It belonged to Uncle Bill!

Tommie struggled into her clothes. She heard her father getting up and lighting the lamp.

"Something must have happened," she heard Mamma say, "or he wouldn't have come this time of night."

Tommie came into the front room as her father opened the door. Uncle Bill was not alone. He had brought his whole family, even Granny and Grandpa.

"Is anything wrong?" Tommie's mother asked anxiously. "It's late—why, it's after eleven o'clock!"

"Oh, it's just some of Bill's foolishness," Granny said, half grumbling, half laughing as she looked indulgently at her youngest son. "The rest of us were all asleep, and Bill made us get up to come over here. He said he hadn't been able to sleep and was going to come over and see if Tommie would pop him some corn."

"What happened to you, Peanuts?" her uncle laughed. "You look as if somebody had lit a Christmas tree inside you!"

"I feel like Christmas," Tommie said shyly. Then she explained about the trip the next day and how she needed a way home after it was over. She didn't tell about her prayer and how he was the answer to it. That was too precious to share with anyone yet. She needed to think about it.

"Why, sure, Peanuts," her uncle said, "I'll come for you to-morrow night. That is, if you'll pop that popcorn I came over here after."

"Uncle Bill," Tommie said fervently, "I'll pop you a whole bushel of popcorn!"

"Better get started, then," he teased. "That's going to take a while."

Tommie hurried into the kitchen and began building up the fire. Then she stopped. She should say Thank You.

"God, I'm so glad to find that You really do answer prayers. Thank You so much. If You answer prayers, You must care about me. Someday I hope to find out more about You. Thank You again. Amen."

Later, listening to the voices of the family in the front room, and to the pop-snap of the popcorn in the pan she manipulated, Tommie mused contentedly. "Perhaps," she thought, "what I have just discovered about God will make a big change in my life."

A Promise of Something Better

"Tommie, there's a magazine for you on the table. It came in the mail today," Mother said as Tommie came in from school.

Tommie slipped the wrapper off the magazine. "It's called *The Youth's Instructor*, Mamma," she said. "I wonder who sent it to me."

"Your Aunt Marty probably subscribed to it for you. It looks like it's published by that Seventh-day Adventist Church she belongs to. I don't much like your reading that Adventist material, but then, I guess it's better than the trash some of your classmates read."

Tommie settled back in her chair with the magazine. One of the stories caught her interest, then another. The stories were good stories, she thought—nothing like what was in the magazines the other girls brought to school. Mother would never let Tommie read them.

"Well," Tommie thought to herself, "Mamma surely can't find anything to object to in this paper. It is all about the Bible and being good. It even has a Bible lesson in it. I wish we had a Bible."

Tommie waited eagerly for the magazine to arrive each week. More and more she wished for a Bible to prove what she read in the *Instructor*.

One day at recess the eighth-grade girls' conversation turned to religion.

"I'm a Methodist," Carolyn declared.

"I go to the Baptist church," said Viola.

"What church do you belong to, Tommie?" asked Reatha.

"I don't belong to any church right now," Tommie said slowly, "but when I get older I'm going to join the Seventh-day Adventist Church."

"I never heard of that church," said Margaret. "What do they believe?"

"They keep the seventh day for Sabbath," replied Tommie.

"The seventh day? But that's Saturday! Nobody goes to church on Saturday!" Viola exclaimed.

"Why do they do that? They must be all mixed up!" chimed in Lorraine.

"It's in the Bible," Tommie said defensively.

"I'll bet it isn't! The Bible says to keep Sunday. I know it does," said Carolyn.

"If you'll bring your Bible to school tomorrow I'll show you where it tells about the Sabbath!" Tommie replied.

"All right, that's just what I'll do," Carolyn said.

That night Tommie looked through her carefully kept copies of *The Youth's Instructor* and marked down all the texts she could find about the Sabbath. The next morning as the bell rang, Carolyn slipped Tommie a small Bible and whispered, "Here it is. At recess we'll see if you can prove your religion!"

Every spare moment until recess Tommie examined the Bible. She had never had one in her hands before, and she had difficulty finding the texts she needed. However, she did locate two of them by the time recess came, and the girls crowded around to hear what she had to say.

"All right, Tommie. Let's hear you prove your Sabbath," Viola said.

"Well, here's a verse in Exodus," Tommie began. "It is Exodus twenty, verses eight, nine, and ten. 'Remember the Sabbath day, to keep it holy. Six days shalt thou labor, and do all thy work, but the seventh day is the Sabbath of the Lord thy God.' That's part of the Ten Commandments."

"But that's in the Old Testament," protested Carolyn, who seemed more familiar with the Bible than the other girls. "We don't go by the Old Testament anymore."

"We don't?" Tommie asked. "Are you sure? Why don't we? It's part of the Bible."

Carolyn hesitated a moment, then confessed, "I'm not sure why, but I know people go mostly by the New Testament these days."

Just then the class bell rang. Tommie whispered hurriedly, "Carolyn, may I borrow your Bible until school is out today?"

"Of course," Carolyn whispered back. "Just get it back to me before I go home this afternoon."

The rest of the day Tommie read Carolyn's Bible during every spare minute. The other girls often saw her engrossed in a book, so they weren't surprised when she didn't join them at noon to play.

Since Carolyn said that people didn't much believe in the Old Testament anymore, Tommie started reading the New Testament. She wasn't half through Matthew when it was time to give the precious Book back to Carolyn.

"Carolyn," Tommie said as she returned the Bible, "if you will bring this back to school tomorrow, I will show you where it says we are not to eat pork."

"Not eat pork?" Carolyn exclaimed. "I never heard of such a thing. Viola, did you hear that? Tommie says the Bible tells us not to eat pork!"

"That's probably in the Old Testament, too." Viola laughed.

"Just the same, I'm going to give Tommie a chance to show me," Carolyn replied.

The next day Tommie again found the texts she wanted and read them to the girls at recess; then she borrowed the Bible until the end of the day. On another day she borrowed Viola's Bible to show the girls that Jesus was coming back to earth. By the end of two weeks, Tommie had borrowed Bibles often enough to read halfway through the book of Acts. Margaret promised to bring her Bible the next Monday so Tommie could show them about paying tithe, and Tommie hoped to read several more chapters in Acts.

"Did you bring your Bible?" Tommie asked Margaret when they got to school Monday.

"No. I'll tell you why at recess. It's time for the bell now," Margaret replied.

The girls acted unusually solemn at recess as they gathered around Tommie.

"I'm sorry, Tommie," Margaret began. "My mother wouldn't let me bring my Bible. She says for me not to discuss religion with you again."

"My mother says you are just confusing us," said Lucinda, who hadn't taken a very active part in the discussions.

"I asked my daddy about the seventh-day Sabbath, and he says you don't understand it all yourself, and for me not to listen to you anymore." This from Lorraine.

Tommie stood speechless for a moment. She had not foreseen this complication.

Lucinda put her arm around her and said with a smile, "Oh, come on, Tommie. We all love you, even if we don't agree with your religion. We can talk about something else. Besides, you haven't been out to play with us at recess for ages. Let's go play ball!"

"All right," Tommie said halfheartedly. She had so wanted to see what happened to Paul in the second half of the book of Acts, but now it might be months, even years, before she got to read the Bible again. But she would still have the *Instructor* each week. Maybe someday she could find out from that the answers to her questions.

Several weeks passed. Then one evening Tommie got off the school bus to find Daddy gone and Mamma giving the orders for evening chores. "Your grandma, Daddy's mother, died this afternoon. Daddy has gone and won't be back until after the funeral," Mamma said.

Daddy's mother had been one of the Adventist relatives. Tommie had not seen this grandma very many times, but she felt grieved to know she was gone. When Daddy returned three days later, he brought with him a box of books that had belonged to his mother.

"Here, Tommie," he said. "You may have these. You're the one who likes to read. I haven't looked through them, but you'll find something interesting. Your grandma liked to read too."

As Tommie started looking through the books she realized with a thrill that these had been Grandma's Adventist books. She recognized many titles she had seen in the *Instructor*. There were *The Desire of Ages*, *Christ Object Lessons*, and others. Grandma had read them so much they had literally fallen to pieces. None had a cover, and most of them were minus front and back chapters, but to Tommie they were a treasure beyond compare.

Near the bottom of the box she came upon something that made her cry out with joy. She found tattered remnants of a Bible! Before exploring further, Tommie sat down on the floor and read the last half of the book of Acts. Then she continued unpacking the box, and the main thing of interest that was left was part of a hymnal.

Tommie used the Bible every day to look up texts she found in the *Instructor*. But some texts she couldn't find because the books before Deuteronomy and after First Peter were missing from Grandma's Bible.

The end of Tommie's grammar-school days drew near. One day the teacher announced, "It is time we began making plans for graduation. None of you will be surprised to learn that Tommie, because of her consistently high grades, will be class valedictorian."

"Oh-h-h," cried Lucinda, throwing her arms around Tommie, "we knew you'd be the one!"

"The rest of us never had a chance, with a bookworm like Tommie in the class," said Margaret.

"Why, she even finds the Bible interesting to read," remarked Viola. Then she laughed, and holding up her hands in mock defense, she said, "Now, Tommie, just because I mentioned the Bible doesn't mean you can talk religion to me!"

But Tommie felt too happy even to reply. Valedictorian of the class! That had been her ambition at the beginning of the school year. Then she had become interested in the Bible and had forgotten about the reward for the highest-ranking eighth-grader.

When the students settled down, the teacher continued, "The graduation exercises will be two weeks from this coming Friday night, and—"

Just then Larry's hand shot up and began to wave wildly. "Yes, Larry, do you have a question you want to ask?"

"Does graduation have to be on Friday night?" he asked. "You see, some people's religion won't let them go to things like graduations on Friday night. My grandma, the one I live with, for one—and—and there are others."

"Why, in that case, Larry, we can have the exercises on Thursday night," the teacher said. "After you finish the county eighth-grade examination on Monday, you will have no more classes this year, so we can have the exercises Thursday night instead of Friday."

Larry's question made Tommie curious. Stopping him in the hall after school that day, she said, "Larry, why did you want our graduation night changed? What religion is your grandmother?"

"She's a Seventh-day Adventist, and I didn't see any sense in graduation being on a night she couldn't come. And then I thought maybe you, too—Tommie, are you an Adventist?"

"Not yet, Larry, but I will be someday. Why did you ask?"

"Oh, I just thought you might be, from the way you talk and act, and the things you read," he answered.

On the way home from school Tommie did some serious thinking. "Larry says I act like an Adventist. But I don't really. I don't even keep the Sabbath. If I only had some way to talk to Adventists, to find out what they're like and more about what they believe. Larry's grandma lives too far away. Daddy would never take me that far. But somehow I'm going to become an Adventist."

Reaching home, Tommie ran eagerly to the house. "Mamma, Mamma!" she called as she reached the door. "Guess what? I'm going to be valedictorian of the class. Isn't that great?"

"Why, Tommie, it's wonderful," Mother said. "But, really, it's no surprise. I never expected anyone but you to be valedictorian. But, I do have a surprise for you."

"Oh, Mamma, what is it?" Tommie squealed, hopping up and down.

"We received a letter today from your aunt Nola. She's invited you to go with her to visit Aunt Marty and Cousin Delores for two weeks. It's sort of a graduation present."

"Do you suppose Daddy will let me go?" Tommie asked.

"Yes, he's already agreed. So if you want to go, it's all settled. You leave the Sunday after graduation. But now it's getting late. You'd better go find the cows."

"Whoopee!" shouted Tommie as she ran outside. This was just what she'd been hoping for. The answer to her prayers. Aunt Nola, Aunt Marty, and Delores were all Seventh-day Adventists. She headed for the south pasture where she expected the cows to be.

"Now I'll have my big chance to see what Adventists are really like," she thought. "I can go to church with them, and I'm sure Delores will help me study the Sabbath School lesson. Maybe Aunt Nola will even know some way I can begin studies for baptism. Now I know that God really is looking out for me."

Then, as she heard the distant tinkling of cowbells coming from the north pasture, she turned and started in a new direction.

We invite you to view the complete
selection of titles we publish at:

www.TEACHServices.com

or write or email us your praises,
reactions, or thoughts about this
or any other book we publish at:

TEACH Services, Inc.
P U B L I S H I N G

www.TEACHServices.com

P.O. Box 954
Ringgold, GA 30736

info@TEACHServices.com

TEACH Services, Inc. titles may be purchased in bulk for
educational, business, fund-raising, or sales promotional use. For
information, please e-mail

BulkSales@TEACHServices.com.

Finally, if you are interested in seeing
your own book in print, please contact us at

publishing@teachservices.com.

We would be happy to review your manuscript for free.

www.ingramcontent.com/pod-product-compliance
Lightning Source LLC
Chambersburg PA
CBHW051839020726
47502CB00005B/1861